CHRONICLES OF V

Broken Stars

TASCHE LAINE

SKYE BLUE PRESS

BROKEN STARS. Copyright © 2024 by Tasche Laine. All rights reserved.

Cover Design by 100 Covers, 100covers.com

ISBN-13: 978-1-955674-55-3 (hardcover)

ISBN-13: 978-1-955674-56-0 (paperback)

ISBN-13: 978-1-955674-57-7 (ebook)

Library of Congress Control Number: 2024903518

Printed in the United States of America

First Edition 2024

Skye Blue Press

Vancouver, WA

https://skyebluepress.com

CONTENTS

For my mother,
whose resilience and grace
taught me strength through loss.
May this story honor the warmth, wisdom,
and unwavering love you've given me,
and be a tribute to
the legacy flowing through our veins.
With all my love and admiration.

In loving memory of
Mary Tallady, my 'Granmary'
February 13, 1919-March 5, 1973

"We do not 'get over' a death. We learn to carry the grief and integrate the loss in our lives. In our hearts, we carry those who have died. We grieve and we love. We remember."

— NATHALIE HIMMELRICH

I

EPIC KISS

My auburn hair cascaded down as I stood on my tiptoes, heart pounding with the thrill of the impending moment. Zack's breath, mint-fresh, fluttered over my lips, drawing us closer in the secluded corner of the school hallway. That summer, Zack had become my anchor, a steady presence while Mom battled her health storms. He was my daily infusion of joy, the single ray of hope in my cloudy sky.

"Seriously, guys? Public display much?" Emma's teasing voice broke through our little world. She gave us a playful shove, her giggle echoing off the lockers.

I teetered, bracing for the smack of the cold tile floor, but Zack's reflexes were on point. His arms, firm and reassuring, circled me, pulling me back from the edge of embarrassment. His eyes, a mix of the ocean and the sky on a clear day, locked with bright green eyes, sparking with that playful challenge we always seemed to share. The tight spiral curls of his dark brown hair bounced with the swift movement; his casual style, a perfect blend of skater meets band tee, somehow just worked, making him stand out without even trying.

"You're the best," I said, half-mocking, half-sincere, grateful for the save yet amused at the over-dramatic rescue.

Emma, with her effortless cool and the kind of vibe that made you think of summer playlists and beach bonfires, rolled her brown eyes so hard I thought they might get stuck. "Can't believe I'm third-wheeling on the first day back," she sighed, but her smile said she didn't mind all that much.

As Zack righted me, ensuring I was steady, I dusted off my jeans, more out of habit than necessity. "Gotta jet to class," Emma threw over her shoulder, already disappearing into the crowd.

Left alone with Zack, the bubble of our moment was popped and replaced by the buzzing anticipation of the day ahead. "We should head to class, too," he murmured, his voice low, just for me.

"Yeah, definitely," I agreed, the electric touch of his hand sending a shiver down my spine.

"See you in APUSH, bae," he said, the corners of his mouth turning up in a promise of more moments like this. "Can't wait."

"Can't wait," I echoed, my heart doing a little dance. "Don't let my mom's class get to you too much, Zee."

He shot back with a grin, "No promises," and with a final squeeze of my hand, he was off.

I watched him go, a silly grin plastered on my face, before turning to confront my own day. Junior year at Sierra High was already shaping up to be one for the books.

★ ★ ★ ★ ★

As I navigated the frenzied hallways of high school, the cacophony of slamming lockers and boisterous chatter faded to a distant hum. An unexpected citrus scent in the air took me back to the orange groves bordering the Tustin Disc Golf Course. I allowed my mind to drift, to wander along the sweet currents of memory—my first kiss with Zack.

It was an uncharacteristically chilly February evening in southern California, barely two weeks into our blossoming relationship. We had just wrapped up a spirited game of Frisbee golf, a challenge Zack issued with a playful twinkle in his eye upon discovering my well-honed Frisbee prowess. Skills that had, under far more dire circumstances on my last case, become my saving grace in the middle of a gang conflict. But that adrenaline-fueled tale was for another day.

Back to that cool evening . . . Our game had ended in my victory, a playful triumph Zack conceded with a grin. As we sauntered back to our bikes, the waning light painted the sky in strokes of lavender and peach, our path lit by the soft glow of the setting sun. Zack reached for my hand, his fingers weaving through mine in a gentle clasp, sending a spark of electricity up my arm. Glancing shyly at him, I saw his silhouette, a dark outline against the dimming sky, but it was enough to quicken my pulse with anticipation.

The night before, Zack had confessed his feelings for me— that he'd been in love with me for over a year. It was a revelation that stopped just short of a kiss. The moment now hung between us, insistent.

There I stood, heart drumming a rapid beat, wondering whether tonight would grant that elusive kiss. As if tuned to the rhythm of my thoughts, Zack leaned in, his lips brushing against mine with a touch so featherlight I might have imagined it. He turned me to face him, his hands cradling my cheeks with a tender yet deliberate motion and kissed me once more. This kiss was different—confident, deep, a promise rather than a question. I wrapped my arms around his neck, surrendering to the moment.

When we finally parted, both of us whispered a breathless, "Wow."

Zack's eyes gleamed with the innocent triumph of first love. "Best. First. Kiss. Ever!"

"Magic," I breathed out in agreement, fingertips lingering on my lips as if to capture the sensation, to etch it into memory.

Yet, amid the magical moment, a shadow flickered; a memory of a first kiss that was anything but enchanting, stolen at a party by someone who didn't matter. I shook off the ghost of that memory, refocusing on this magical night. With Zack, every nuanced touch redefined what a first kiss should be—genuine, thrilling, and filled with the promise of tomorrow.

It marked the beginning of something truly epic. There I was—Violet Hemingway Jiménez—embarking on a journey I never expected. I had a boyfriend!

As I took my seat in Mr. Sutton's class, a part of me still wondered when I would wake up from this beautiful dream.

2

EARLY BIRD SATS?

The bell's screeching sound snapped me back to reality. Instant panic—I'd spaced out the whole first period. Mr. Sutton's math spiel on logs and derivatives might as well have been in another language. Math? Not my thing, and Pre-Calc was shaping up to be a nightmare. How did I even get here? Last year, Zack pretty much saved me in Algebra 2. Without his tutoring, I'd have been lost. Even with his help, pulling off a C felt like climbing Mount Everest.

I shoved my books into my bag, maybe a tad too energetically, and headed straight for APUSH (AP US History). Just thinking about that class got my heart racing, and not 'cause I'm some history buff. It was all about Zack being there.

Entering the classroom, I spotted him instantly. Zack's grin cut through the crowd, guiding me through the sea of desks. He casually knocked his backpack off the next chair, saving me a spot. My face heated up as I took my seat, feeling like every little thing between us was still fresh and exciting, even seven months into being "us." Last year, Comp Sci's strict seating had kept us apart, but now, in this new first, we were side by side.

"Is it super weird having my mom as your English teacher?" I whispered, leaning in a bit.

"Weird? Nah," he whispered back, a grin in his voice. "Your mom's actually hilarious. Those puns she drops? Comedy gold. Honestly, I'm kinda psyched for her class."

His words caught me off guard. A mix of pride and a weird twinge of something else . . . jealousy? Nah, couldn't be. I let out a silent breath, shaking the feeling away like an unwelcome chill.

Mr. Fox, our APUSH teacher, was like a celeb at Sierra High. Young, sharp, and shrouded in school gossip, he was as much a character as the historical figures we studied. And being the kid of two of the most well-known teachers at school? Yeah, talk about a double-edged sword.

Sometimes I joked about wanting to be shipped off to some Hogwarts-esque boarding school just to escape the constant "teachers' kid" spotlight. But deep down, I wasn't looking for an escape. I loved my parents too much. Still, being in the spotlight all the time, especially with Mom's health battles, was getting heavier by the day.

When Mom first got sick, they thought surgery had nixed the cancer for good. But cancer's tricky like that, always lurking. And so, the whispers and pitying looks followed me around, slicing through me sharper than any harsh word ever could. I wasn't looking for their sympathy; I just wanted things to be normal, for Mom to be okay.

FINALLY, lunch rolled around. I zipped across the quad, ready to snag our favorite table under the giant shade tree. In August's heatwave, finding some shade was like finding a treasure.

"V! This way," Emma shouted, waving me over.

I paused, spotting her at a table dead center in the quad, zero shade in sight. "What's up with ditching our usual spot? You know I like to stay on the fringe," I half-joked, half-whined as I walked up.

"Last year's spot is old news," she shrugged, like that explained everything.

"But—"

Zack cut in as he joined us, "Why're we camping out here in the sun?"

"Exactly my point," I backed up, but Emma was quick to dismiss us.

"Let's drop it, okay? We've got more important matters to address," she insisted, brushing off the table drama.

Zack and I exchanged a look, then turned to Emma, signaling her to spill it. "What's up?" he nudged.

Emma leaned in, excitement clear in her voice. "So, last night Coach Marley told my mom a UNC scout's coming to our first game! Can you believe it? I was like, 'Why the first game? And I'm just a junior.' But mom said that's how they roll, scouting early and all."

I blinked, totally lost. "UNC? Which one's that again?"

Emma gave me a you've-got-to-be-kidding look. "University of North Carolina at Chapel Hill. It's huge in women's soccer. Mia Hamm ring a bell?"

I drew a blank, which only amped up her shock. "Mia Hamm, soccer icon? My room's basically a shrine to her, V!"

"Oh, right, that Mia Hamm," I fumbled, trying to play it cool.

"Anyway, imagine me walking the same halls as Mia Hamm!" Emma was practically bouncing. "Mom said they even look at freshmen. Crazy, right? And my guidance counselor was like, 'Aim for a 1470 on the SATs for scholarships.'"

"So, brains and brawn, huh?" Zack said with a playful wink.

Emma and I rolled our eyes, but she was quick to get back on track. "Yeah, I gotta hit the SAT books soon. Taking it next month."

"Next month? Isn't that early?" Zack leaned in, curious.

Emma explained her game plan, "I did the PSAT thing, but gotta see where I stand with the real deal. Then maybe retake it after some serious study time."

I exhaled, feeling for her. "That's intense, Em. Super glad I'm not in those shoes." Wanting to shift gears, I added, "Can we shelf the college talk for today? It's just day one, let's live a little."

Emma looked sheepish. "You're right. This year does feel different, doesn't it?"

"No kidding," I said, raising an eyebrow for emphasis.

Zack, the outsider to our freshman and sophomore year sagas, looked puzzled. "What's the backstory?"

Emma filled him in, "Freshman year was a wild ride for V and me. And last year? V nearly got suspended for a showdown with the principal."

Zack's eyes widened. "Sounds like you two never have a dull moment."

Emma shrugged it off, "It's in the past. We're good now."

Eager to change the subject, I switched gears. "This year, I drove myself to school in my own car, and no drama with Principal Fitz. Pretty cool, right?"

Emma's smile brought a sense of relief, easing the tension. "Yeah, that is pretty cool. Here's to a new year without any drama on the first day. And maybe, one of these days, I'll have my own car too," she said, her tone wistful.

Zack and I exchanged a knowing glance, understanding Emma's situation. In California, the driving laws were strict— no one under twenty in the car unless they were a sibling, and a year's wait was mandatory once we'd had a license. Emma, though licensed, was carless. Her overprotective mother cited a "lack of funds," a reason we all suspected was less about money and more about control.

Zack's part-time job at Skaterz, the local skateboard shop, had earned him enough for an 11-year-old Nissan Pathfinder. He joked about needing the cargo space for his many hobbies, from skateboarding to surfing. I, on the other hand, had my parents to thank. Teachers through and through, they believed my job was solely to be a student, focusing on academia over employment. They insisted work could wait, but good grades couldn't.

The memory of getting my car was still fresh, a highlight of my summer:

The morning of my sixteenth birthday, a navy blue 2012 Subaru Impreza hatchback sat in our driveway, adorned with a massive red bow. My dad chose it for its safety ratings, after hours of extensive research.

I was beyond thrilled to have my own car! My excitement eclipsed my judgment as I'd insisted on taking the driver's test in the Subaru—that very day! This was a poor decision born from overconfidence rather than familiarity with the vehicle.

At the DMV, Emma and I, sharing a birthday, registered for our tests together, as we'd planned years earlier. She, in her mom's familiar sedan, breezed through. I, in my barely-driven Subaru, faltered. A crucial mistake made, misjudging the car's size. I clipped a cone during the parallel parking section. A rookie error, clear and embarrassing.

"FAIL" glared at me from the instructor's clipboard. My

cheeks burned with humiliation, the dream of freedom momentarily dashed. Two weeks later, after many patient hours with my dad, I passed with a relieved grin.

Back at lunch, I smiled at the thought of future escapades. "I can't wait for the day we can all drive somewhere together," I said, brightening. "Road trip, anyone?"

Emma's laugh echoed, the wistfulness replaced by her usual upbeat spirit. "Definitely! As soon as I get my own set of wheels, we're hitting the road!"

"Count me in," Zack chimed in, grinning. "The Pathfinder's up for it."

"So it looks like the only decision left is whose car to take," I teased.

Laughter filled the air as the bell rang, signaling the end of lunch. We gathered our stuff and headed off, promising Emma we'd catch up later. Walking away, I felt this deep sense of gratitude for Zack and Emma. They were more than just my crew; they were my rock. With them, high school felt like an adventure we were all in together.

LUNCH BREAK WAS A WRAP, and only two classes stood between me and calling day one of junior year a win. AP Physics was next on the list, and honestly, I was kind of dreading it. But Zack, being Zack, lightened the mood on our way to class with a classic, corny joke.

"Okay, so why did the scarecrow win an award?"

I braced myself for the cringe. "I have no idea."

"Because he was outstanding in his field . . . get it? Field of matter?"

I tried to stifle a giggle. "That's so bad, it's almost good."

"See? Physics can be a blast," he grinned, giving my hand a quick squeeze before darting off to his own class.

Spoiler alert: Physics was anything but a blast for me. But the day picked up with my last class, Art, which I took partly because, well, I needed an elective and partly because Emma was in it. Classes always feel less like a drag when your bestie's with you.

Mr. Slauson kicked things off with some quick sketch exercises. Surprisingly, I got super into it, diving headfirst into this creative zone I didn't even know I had. It was like unlocking a new level in a game, discovering this hidden talent I had for drawing.

When the final bell rang, it was like a giant exhale after holding my breath all day. Drama-free and in one piece? I'd call that a solid first day.

After school, Emma dashed off to soccer practice, hyped to chat with her coach about the UNC scout, while Zack caught up with me by my locker. "Catch you later," he said after a quick kiss, heading off to Skaterz with that "off to save the world" vibe, though we both knew he lived for that job.

And then it was just me, strolling to the parking lot, heading to MY car. That thought alone had me grinning. No more hitching rides with my parents. This car was my ticket to freedom, my own little slice of the open road. Day one of junior year? Nailed it.

* ★ ★ ★ ★

THE HOUSE WAS EERILY silent when I walked in, the quiet broken only by Lucky's excited barks. "What's up, Lucky?" I gave him the usual ear scratches. "Looks like it's just you and me, buddy."

Lucky, our energetic Yorkie-Pom mix with his patchwork of tan, black, and white fur, had quickly become a core part of our family. Suzie, who volunteered at a pet rescue, hooked us up with him after Scotty, my little brother, launched a full-blown puppy campaign last year. Now, Lucky was as much a Jiménez as any of us.

The silence was uncharacteristic. Our home was usually a whirlwind of activity, a sharp contrast to my need for some alone time. I'd usually be camped out in my room with a book or some tunes, but today, the kitchen felt more inviting. Flipping through the mail, mostly bills, my heart skipped a beat when I saw an envelope from Dr. Khatri, Mom's oncologist. It was like a stark reminder of the medical marathon she'd been running.

The series of treatments, the surgeries—it was a landscape of interventions I had tried to block out. Her first surgery, the double mastectomy, was two years ago. Then last spring, they removed her ovaries, a polyp on her uterus, and a fibroid tumor.

Our usual summer adventures had been hijacked by cancer, with Mom's immunity too compromised for travel. My family was all about those budget-friendly travel hacks, hitting up new states or even countries—every trip bigger and better than the last. But this summer, Mom had to sit it out, the chemo and radiation taking their toll. She took the summer to rest, to build up her immune system again, and to get her strength back up.

Despite everything, Mom was a fighter. Just two weeks before school started, she was all set to go back to teaching, rocking a new short, curly hairstyle that was even redder than before, making her look even more fierce.

I put the bills aside, tossed out the junk mail, and whipped up some peanut butter toast for a snack. I was mid-bite when Scotty burst in, with all the energy of an eight-year-old. "V! You won't believe what I did today!"

"Hey, Scott-o! How's the third-grade life treating ya?" I shot back, trying out a new nickname on him.

He made a face, ruffling his spiky blond hair. "Scott-o?"

I laughed. "Yeah, you know, after you vetoed 'squirt' and 'mini-troll.' Yay or nay?"

Mom walked in then, her arms full of school stuff, looking a bit worn but with that same spark in her fern-green eyes. "Trying out new nicknames again?" she teased.

I rushed over to help her with the files. "You okay, Mom? First day back got you beat?"

She laughed, that familiar, warm sound filling the kitchen. "It's the good kind of beat," she said, her smile telling me she wouldn't have it any other way.

"Hey, what about my day!" Scotty piped up, practically bouncing with the need to share his news.

"Alright, hit me with it, little dude," I said. "What's your big news?"

"I won a class scavenger hunt! I get to pick any book I want from the library!" he beamed.

"That's awesome, bookworm!" I said, tousling his hair.

Scotty ducked away. "Just Scotty, okay?"

"As you wish, Scotty," I replied with a mock bow.

"That's better." He grinned. "Mom, can I take Lucky outside and play fetch?"

"May I," Mom corrected, ever the teacher.

"Right, right, May I?" Scotty asked again.

"Yes, but stay in the backyard, and don't open the gate for any reason. Oh, make sure his collar is on. Remember what happened last time?"

"Okay, okay," Scotty said, rolling his eyes. "Got it."

"Eye-rolling at your mom? Bold move, son," Mom quipped, her eyes alight with mischief.

"Maybe?" Scotty said, unsure.

"Here comes the tickle monster—"

Scotty's eyes went wide, "I'm outta here?" he declared, dashing off with Lucky before the tickle threat could become reality.

Mom and I watched them play for a bit, then I brought it up again. "Seriously though, are you really okay?"

She sank into a chair, a sigh escaping her. "Today was . . . a lot. First, I had to convince everyone I'm fit to teach again. They were surprised to see me back so soon. But I jumped right into the fray, getting back into the swing of things. It felt right, like slipping back into my favorite pair of jeans."

I handed her a glass of water. "Does that mean you had a good day?"

"Yep, I sure did. It was a thrill to still be a part of the scramble to get ready for a new school year. You know, it might sound strange, but it felt like a blessing to feel like I'm such a normal part of the routine again. It felt like coming home. It was wonderful." She smiled and added, "And of course, I promptly fell in love with all my new students."

"You say that every year," I pointed out, half-joking.

"I mean it every year! I truly love my students, and I love teaching. Every year."

"I know you do, Mom. They're lucky to have you." I paused and took a deep breath, "Okay, gotta ask—how's Zack doing in your AP Lit class? Be honest, is he causing trouble?"

Her smile didn't falter. "Your guy's sharp, V. Really adds to the class. You chose well."

I felt a blush warm my cheeks. "Cool. Thanks, Mom."

3
EMMA'S QUEST

At lunch the next day, Emma thrust a glossy brochure into my hands. I scanned it to see what had her so excited.

PREPPED: **Empowering Success Through Preparation!**

- The only course you need to prepare for the SAT!
- Guaranteed to improve your score or you don't pay!
- Learn key strategies and techniques to make test day a breeze!
- Includes 4 full-length practice tests!
- Have test anxiety? Worry no more! Our test-taking tips will ensure your success!
- Get accepted to your college of choice—enroll today!

"Emma, we talked about this yesterday," I said, shaking my

head. I tossed the slick ad onto the table like it had sprouted fangs. "I said I'll take the test in the spring."

"I know that's what you said but hear me out. Please." She paused, her eyes begging for a chance to plead her case.

I stared at her a moment, then gave in with a slight nod. Folding my arms across my chest, I prepared for her pitch.

"As you know, my counselor thinks it's a good idea for me to take the test early, like next month. By taking it early, I'll gain an advantage in applying for scholarships. Hardly any juniors apply this early, and if I wait until next year, it might be too late. So, by taking this test prep course together, we could turn this stressful, scary thing into something kinda fun. It would benefit both of us, and we could help each other stay motivated, you know, be each other's study buddies and then we can celebrate when we *both* get into our dream schools! The class meets every Saturday morning, plus Thursday nights for practice tests, spread out over a month. We'll be ready to take the test the first Saturday in October. If you take the exam with me, you'll get it out of the way, and have one less thing to do later." She smiled, hopeful.

I narrowed my eyes, feeling ambushed. "You've had this speech prepared, haven't you?"

Emma shifted uncomfortably but was about to respond when Zack strolled up to our table, his tray a mountain of cafeteria grub. "Hey there, stunners!" he greeted, but his grin faded a bit seeing our serious faces. "What's up?"

"Emma's on a mission to get me to sacrifice every Saturday for SAT prep," I said.

"It's not the whole day, chill," Emma countered. "You'd still have your afternoons free, and it's only for a month."

"Guess it's one way to make sure you don't sleep away the weekend," Zack joked.

Rolling my eyes, I brushed my hair aside. "But what if I'm not even ready for that test? Might be stuff on it I haven't learned in class yet."

"Seriously?" Zack said between bites. "You know you can take it more than once, right? Aim higher each time."

"And why would I torture myself with a marathon test over and over if I don't absolutely have to?" I shot back.

Zack just shrugged, his mouth full.

Leaning in, Emma's eyes lit up with an idea. "Why don't you jump on the early SAT train with us, Zack?"

He looked like a deer caught between the headlights, gulping down his bite. "Work's slammed on Saturdays for me, so maybe next fall. Plus, I'm eyeing community college first, keep the costs low, ya know? Just me and my mom on this."

I felt my cheeks heat up. "Hey, having a college fund at the ready wasn't my call. My parents just always assumed I'd head that way."

Emma, always curious, asked, "What about your dad? Can he chip in for college?" Zack's dad was a bit of a mystery to her, especially since her own dad had been a hero who never made it home a few months after she was born.

"Yeah, he does what he can, helps out with child support and stuff. But he's all over the map with construction gigs, hardly ever home."

"Sounds tough," Emma sympathized.

Zack shrugged it off. "Nah, I'm used to it. Always been that way."

Feeling a bit sidelined by their chat, I let out an exaggerated sighed. "Alright, alright, I'm in. I'll take the Prepped course with you. I guess I'll take the SAT early, too."

Emma practically jumped for joy. "Trust me, it'll be fun! I'll whip us up a study plan that's actually doable. Leave it to me, I got this."

Despite myself, I cracked a smile. Turning down Emma wasn't really an option.

By Friday, Emma had enrolled us in the Prepped course that started early the next morning. But I didn't want to think about that now, it was Labor Day weekend and I had a fun date planned with Zack. We were going to the Street Fair in Old Towne Orange.

The street lights and twinkling colors of the displays of handmade crafts, jewelry, and art cast a warm glow over everything, turning the night bright and festive. Music played in the background from one of the many stages set up for live entertainment. As Zack and I wandered between the game stalls, he looked determined to conquer something. A smile crept across my face. It was typical of him to dive into things with full enthusiasm.

Zack zeroed in on a classic carnival challenge, the old "knock down the pyramid of cans" game. We paused in front of the booth, and he flashed me a confident grin. "Check this out," he declared, sliding a five to the booth guy as he prepared for his first shot.

But, as it turned out, those cans were stubborn. His initial toss didn't even graze them, veering off dramatically. He shot me a sheepish look, but I was all about the hype, encouraging him to give it another go.

With each attempt, he inched closer and closer until, finally, the cans clattered down in defeat. The booth attendant, with a nonchalant wave, invited Zack to pick his prize. Scanning the options, Zack's eyes lit up as he nabbed a plushie.

Handing it over, he was all smiles. "Cute, huh?"

"It's awesome," I said, genuinely touched, giving the plush Pit Bull a squeeze. It was white with charming brown patches and those irresistibly droopy ears.

"So, got a name for it?" Zack asked.

"Backup," I said, instantly sure.

He paused, a bit confused, then his face brightened. "Oh, like the dog from your favorite TV show 'Veronica Mars'?"

"Exactly!" His recall of my all-time favorite series—and its loyal dog, Backup—warmed my heart. "You get me," I added, feeling that familiar rush of affection for him.

Zack's grin grew as he wrapped an arm around me, pulling me in as we meandered through the fair. Clutching my new plushie, I felt this perfect sense of belonging. The fair was alive around us, but in that moment, it felt like we were in our own cozy bubble.

By 8 AM the next morning, I was zombie-walking toward the Orange Public Library, which didn't officially open its doors until 10. But there we were, a bunch of us gathered for the Prepped SAT course, waiting to be let in for our early morning brain workout.

Emma spotted me first, her energy level somehow at a hundred percent. Her black ponytail was practically vibrating with excitement. "Morning, sunshine!" she chirped, bouncing on the balls of her feet.

My sarcasm went unchecked as I hissed through gritted

teeth, "Easy there, it's not like we're front row at a Taylor Swift show." Jacob caught my eye as he openly stared at Emma. He'd been in my freshman geometry class and was a known class clown, so seeing him here, of all places, was weird. And, why was he eyeing Emma like that? He creeped me out.

Emma just laughed off my morning mood, oblivious of Jacob. "Still not a fan of mornings, huh? Scotty still calling you 'Grouchy Bear'?"

I shot her a look. "Only on his brave days."

She giggled, unfazed. "As if you'd ever really chase him down."

"Whatever. Can we not bring my brother into this? Are we getting in or what?" I grumbled, more awake now but questioning my life choices that led to SAT prep at dawn.

The atmosphere was unexpectedly lively for such an ungodly hour, making me think this SAT thing might just be more of an adventure than I'd bargained for.

DRIVING HOME after that first SAT prep class, I had to admit Emma was onto something. The session was surprisingly legit, loaded with solid test hacks. And Lucas Bennett, the instructor? Guy had a knack for keeping things light, cracking jokes that actually made the morning bearable.

But then there was Jacob, self-appointed ruler of the back-row bandits, chatting away like we were at some social club. He talked to the others around him the whole time. It was beyond irritating, more like a huge distraction. Yet, what blew my mind was Mr. Bennett's obliviousness to Jacob's non-stop chatter. He was totally clueless. Either he was fresh meat in the teaching game or just too chill to bother. He looked young enough to be mistaken for a senior rather than the one running the show.

I thought about going full-on 'Mom-mode' on Jacob, channeling her teacher vibes to shut down his side show. But, I didn't want to cause drama on day one. So, I bit my tongue and rode out the chatter.

Still, I couldn't figure out why Jacob was even there. Like Emma and me, he was a junior. Emma had her reasons to take the SATs early, but Jacob? He was a C average student—at best —whose track record screamed more 'party planner' than 'academic achiever.' Everyone else in the class were seniors, a diverse mix from the high schools in our area—thirty-two, by my count.

My phone pinged with a text from Mom, breaking my train of thought. No way was I checking it while behind the wheel, though. Safety first. Once parked at home, I saw her message lighting up the screen:

MOM

Big day alert! I'm celebrating one more year of being above ground—very informally, but very happily! It's been two years since my diagnosis 'D-day!' If you can, even for 15 minutes, stop by Haven's this Monday (Sept 4, my b-day) between 6:30-10 p.m. I'd love to see you and drink a beer with you! I know it's Labor Day so no worries if you have other plans. It's always last minute with us. But who knows? Sometimes the BEST gatherings are. 😊

4

ANOTHER YEAR ABOVE GROUND

Lucky greeted me as I walked in the front door. "Hey, buddy." I patted his head. "Where's Mom?" I walked into the living room, trailed by Lucky. After a quick search of the kitchen, I shouted, "Mom?"

"Up here, sweetie," her voice wafted down from upstairs.

I bounded up the stairs, two at a time with Lucky at my heels. We entered Mom's bedroom without knocking. "Where are Dad and Scotty?"

"Soccer," she replied from her bedroom closet. "How was your class?"

"Oh yeah, soccer. Duh." Lucky jumped up on Mom's bed and I joined him, scratching him behind the ears. "Class was cool. I already picked up a few worthy test-taking tips, but that's not what I want to talk about. On my way home, I got a strange text from you. It was about going to a bar and drinking beer together."

Mom chuckled, walking out of the closet with an empty hanger in her hand. "Oopsie, hee hee. I guess my multi-tasking skills could use some work. I was texting while folding laundry and accidentally sent you that invite. I thought I'd plan a little impromptu birthday party, invite some friends to celebrate another year above—"

I interrupted, thrusting my hand out as though I could control any of this simply by silencing her next words. "Don't say it. You know I can't stand that phrase. *Another year above ground.* It's . . . unsettling. But never mind that. Why did you invite me to a bar? You know I can't drink there."

Mom sighed, her tone playful, "I told you, that invite wasn't meant for you. That's what I get for trying to multi-task. And for the record, you can't drink alcohol at a bar or in a car, not here or there, not anywhere."

I laughed, giving her a knowing look. "Very funny, Sam-I-Am. You know I've always had a soft spot for Dr. Seuss. But seriously, why do you say that every year?"

Mom paused for a moment, her expression turning thoughtful. "Say what?"

"The 'above the ground' thing. It creeps me out," I admitted.

She nodded, her voice taking on a more serious tone. "Well, sweetie, it's better than the alternative . . . being six feet underground. I celebrate because the more birthdays I have, the longer I'm still here. Still breathing. Still fighting. Still living."

The weight of the world seemed to crash down on me. "But what does that mean? You're sick again? I thought you were getting better!"

Mom paused, and I could almost hear my heart pounding over the silence. "Mom, no! Why do you always wait till the last minute to tell me this stuff? I don't understand . . . you just went back to work."

Her eyes were glossy, voice shaky. "I just . . . didn't want to burden you."

That was it—I hit my breaking point. "Seriously? Mom,

you're not some kind of burden. And hello, I'm not five anymore. You don't need to sugarcoat things or keep me in the dark. Stop the lies. It's like everyone thinks keeping secrets from kids makes things better, but NO, we just want the straight-up truth."

She let out a heavy sigh, looking defeated. "Alright, the real deal then." She sat on the bed next to me, taking my hand. "I'm not exactly sick again. It's just . . . the doctors found some irregularities in my latest checkup and got a bit worried."

My stomach did a dive. "Worried? What are the 'irregularities'?"

Mom took a big gulp of air, like she was about to dive into cold water or something and then plunged in. "It means they're just keeping a close eye on things. The cancer hasn't come back, but there's always a chance it could. I don't want to worry you over something that might not even happen."

I clung to her hand, caught between freaking out and feeling kind of relieved. "Look, Mom, I know you're trying to protect me, but I need to know what's going on. We're supposed to be in this together, right? Let me be there for you."

Her eyes welled up, but she nodded. "You're absolutely right, sweetheart. We're a team. I promise to be more open with you from now on, no matter how difficult it may be—I'll keep you in the loop."

I brushed away a sneaky tear, forcing a smile. "Good. Thanks, Mom. And hey, your birthday's coming up. Let's do something here at home first, just us—our family. I'll bake a cake for you and make it a special day. Then you can have your big bash with your friends later that night."

Her smile could've lit up the room. "I'd love that. You being here is the best gift I could have, sweetie."

We sat there, side by side, and I made a silent vow to not waste a single moment with her. No matter what was coming, we'd face it together.

GRANDMA SHOWED up around noon the next day, ready to dive into Labor Day weekend and help us throw Mom's family birthday bash. Mom said she wanted some private chat time with Grandma about stuff she didn't want Scotty to overhear, probably her health. She asked me to take Scotty to the park for a while. I didn't mind. The weather was perfect and I was up for catching some rays any chance I got.

"Hey Scotty," I hollered, "wanna go to the park?"

"Yeah! Can Lucky come too?" Scotty replied, with Lucky already doing zoomies.

"Yep. Grab his leash and a ball. Maybe we can play catch if it's not too crowded."

Scotty happily fetched Lucky's leash and a ball, and we were on our way. I basked in the sun-bathed sidewalks as we headed to the park. A slight breeze blew through my hair as the palm trees swayed around us; it was a perfect day for an afternoon in the park.

After about half an hour of throwing the ball for Lucky, Scotty said, "I'm hot, thirsty, and tired. Can we go home now?"

"Good call. I should have brought a couple waters with us. Sorry, bro, my bad." I glanced at our panting pup. "Looks like Lucky's thirsty, too. Come on, let's go."

On our walk home, Lucky, normally only interested in squirrels, began throwing glances behind us. I glanced that direction and saw a man wearing a baseball cap about a block back. Usually, I wouldn't care. We always saw people around on our walks. But Lucky's unusual behavior had me concerned.

"V, do you see that man?" Scotty asked, a hint of worry in his voice. "Lucky keeps looking at him. He's never done that before."

"Yeah, I see him. He's probably enjoying the beautiful day, out on a walk, just like us."

But Scotty wasn't convinced. His furrowed brow and tightened grip on Lucky's leash told me his young mind was racing with worrisome thoughts. "But what if he's not? What if he's a bad, scary man?"

I wanted to laugh off his fears, to tell him he was being silly, but our dog was practically walking backward, he was straining so hard to keep his eyes on the man behind us. It was beginning to freak me out too.

"Let's pick up the pace a bit, yeah?" I suggested, more for my own growing unease than for Scotty's.

We power-walked the rest of the way, the sound of our footsteps brisk against the pavement. I stole another glance behind us. The man was still there, maintaining the same distance. A chill ran down my spine despite the hot day.

Lucky's odd behavior only increased. His ears perked up, his head turned back every few seconds. Was it a scent he picked up? Was there something sinister about this man?

"V, I'm scared," Scotty whispered, his eyes wide with fear.

I squeezed his hand for reassurance. "It's okay, Scotty. We're almost home." But even as I said it, doubt crept into my mind. What if Scotty's fears were not unfounded? What if there was a real reason for Lucky's distress?

We rounded the corner, the familiar sight of our house

coming into view. I risked one last glance back. The man was gone, vanished as if he'd never been there.

At once, Lucky relaxed and resumed his usual carefree trot. Scotty let out a long breath, his earlier fear melting away under the comforting sunshine.

Once safe at home, I couldn't shake off the heebie-jeebies. What was that all about? For now, though, I was just happy to be back in our own space, drama-free.

✶ ✶ ✶ ✶ ✶

THE AFTERNOON SUN cast a golden glow over the living room, now transformed into a cozy celebration space for Mom's birthday. I did a final walkthrough, ensuring every detail was in place. I wanted everything to be perfect for the party, even though it was just our little family and Grandma. Balloons bobbed in the corners, anchored to the ends of Scotty's colorful handmade banner. The aroma of carrot cake, Mom's favorite, filled the air, promising sweetness to come.

I'd taken on cake duty, determined to nail Grandma's legendary recipe. She guided me through the steps, from grating the carrots to the final flourish of icing that proudly declared, "41 and Fabulous!" It was a labor of love, a tangible piece of the heart I wanted Mom to feel today.

Dad was out back, burger master for the day, while Grandma shared a few of Mom's childhood birthday tales, keeping us in constant giggles.

When everything was ready, Scotty ran upstairs to get Mom. They descended the stairs hand-in-hand, giving me all the feels. As Scotty led her to the armchair, I crowned Mom with a sparkly tiara, playing up the queen-for-a-day treatment. She played along, even throwing in a royal wave for fun.

"Time for presents!" Scotty announced, carrying a small, clumsily wrapped package toward Mom.

"Hold up!" Dad called out, pausing the moment. "We can't do presents without the birthday anthem!"

Everyone gathered around Mom as we raised our voices in a not-so-perfect but heartfelt rendition of the "Happy Birthday" song. The glow in her eyes as she made her wish and blew out the candles was a moment I wished I could freeze in time.

Grandma and I cut and plated the cake while Scotty carefully passed out each slice, bursting with pride that I finally let him help this year. The room buzzed with Scotty's soccer stories, Dad's jokes, Grandma's repeated tales of Mom's childhood, and Mom chiming in with a few stories of her own. I gazed at each member of my family, taking it all in, and a wave of gratitude washed over me.

As the party drew to a close, it was clear that today was more than a celebration of my mother's birthday. I understood why it was so important to her to celebrate birthdays, why she always said that annoying line about being another year above ground. We were celebrating the moment, the joy of being together and being alive. We weren't ignoring the reality of her fragile health, we were savoring the laughter and shared stories, cherishing each precious moment we had together.

When it was time for Mom and Dad to head out to her next celebration, the one at the bar with the beer drinking, Mom pulled me into a hug that felt like a warm blanket. Her voice was a soft whisper, "Thank you, my beautiful angel. This day, this moment with you is imprinted on my heart. I love you beyond words, to the stars and infinity—forever."

"I love you too, Mom; to the stars and infinity—forever."

Watching my parents leave, I felt a mix of happy and heavy, knowing we had this unshakeable bond to keep us steady, come what may. Today was more than just cake and candles; it was about us, our family, facing the ups and downs together.

5
AMANDA

t 8 PM, my phone lit up with Zack's selfie popping up on the screen.

"Sup, Zackster," I answered playfully.

His tone was off though, serious. "Can we talk? Like, in person?"

I checked the time, feeling a twist in my gut. "Yeah, but you know, Grandma's here, and Scotty's on a sugar high . . ."

"I'm already on my way. Be outside in ten?" He hung up before I could even argue.

I bolted downstairs, my mind racing with possibilities. Grandma was in the kitchen with Scotty, making a glass of chocolate milk. "Grandma, Zack's coming over. He sounds upset."

She gave me the 'it's-past-curfew' eyebrow. "It's a little late for a school night, don't you think? Is everything okay?"

"I honestly have no clue. He said he needed to talk, and he sounded worried about something."

Grandma, in her infinite wisdom, was like, "Just talk it out, honey. You know how you teens get with the drama." She gave me a reassuring hug. "I'm sure everything will turn out fine."

"Okay, thanks. I'm gonna go wait for him outside," I said, turning to leave.

Just as I stepped outside, Zack's car pulled up. I got in the car and barely shut my door when he backed out of the driveway, not even waiting for me to buckle up first. I fumbled with the seatbelt and finally clicked it into place. Once the annoying alarm stopped, the rest of our drive was silent—except for my heart thudding in my ears.

Zack finally parked in the middle of nowhere, on some secluded gravel road. He turned to me, his expression solemn. "I've got an older sister."

"I know. I mean, how come you never mentioned her?"

"It's complicated," he mumbled, looking everywhere but at me. "Wait, what do you mean you know?"

It was my turn to avoid his gaze. "Uh, I may have peeked at your student file when I had trust issues last year."

He laughed it off. "Oh really? Typical V, always playing detective, huh?"

"You're not mad?"

"Nah, it's kinda sweet, in a stalker-ish way. You barely talked to me last year. It means you cared enough to dig."

"What if I told you I did it because I was looking for dirt on you?"

He shook his head. "It doesn't matter what your motives were. You finally caved, and now you're my girlfriend."

I playfully punched his arm.

"So, what did the file say about my sister?"

"Not even that much. It just mentioned that you had one sibling. That's it. I forgot about it till just now, actually. I figured if you ever wanted to tell me about her, you would."

"Thanks."

"For what?"

"For loving me. For your patience. I realize I'm not exactly an open book."

"Sure. I know you have your reasons." I hugged him. "Do you want to tell me about her now? I think you started to . . . sorry I got us off track."

"It's okay. I'm glad you told me about the file. It actually makes this easier for me, in a way. We've both kept things from each other."

"Very funny."

"I'm not trying to be funny, V. I don't mean to keep secrets from you. There are just some things that are hard for me to talk about. And Amanda's one of them."

"Amanda is your sister?"

Zack nodded. "Yeah, and she's in trouble." He inhaled deeply, his voice shaky. "My mom was married before she met my dad. She had my half-sister, Amanda. I don't really know her because she moved out when I was little. But tonight, Mom told me Amanda is seriously ill. She needs a bone marrow transplant."

"Oh, Zack, that's terrible. I'm so sorry."

He swallowed hard, his eyes glistening. "They think I might be a match. It's a lot to process. She's practically a stranger, and now I might be the only one who can save her life."

The weight of his revelation was immense. "But what about your parents? Can't one of your parents be the donor? I don't understand why it has to be you."

"I don't get it either, but my dad isn't Amanda's dad. Anyway, I go in for testing tomorrow and I'll find out if I'm a match Wednesday. V, I haven't seen her in forever."

I reached for his hand. "Zack, whatever happens, whatever you decide to do, I'm here for you. We're in this together, okay?"

He gave me a small, grateful smile that kinda broke my heart. "Thanks, V. I just needed someone to talk to. It means a lot that you're here."

As we sat in Zack's car, under the starlit sky, I realized that life was full of unexpected challenges, and my heart hurt for him. All we could do was be there for each other and ride it out together.

Navigating the sterile hospital halls, Zack, his mom Chloe, and I were caught in a silent storm of emotions. Every step Zack took, I could feel his hand squeeze mine a little tighter, like he was trying to ground himself.

We finally reached the designated meeting room, and there she was—Amanda. The Amanda in Chloe's old photos was just a kid; this Amanda, at twenty-six, was all grown up. She held her head high, presenting a mature vibe, with her black hair all business in a bun, and her eyes . . . wow, those eyes had stories, like she'd seen too much but was ready to face more.

By her side was a guy, had to be her husband, and playing at their feet, the cutest twin toddlers I'd ever seen. They were mini Amandas, curious and bright-eyed, soaking up the world.

When Amanda saw Zack, it was like she couldn't believe her brother was right in front of her. "Zack?" Her voice barely made it out.

Zack cleared his throat, trying to keep it together. "Yeah, Mads, it's me."

Hearing that old nickname, something in Amanda just

crumbled, and I could see her fighting back the tears. Chloe stepped forward then, her voice soft but filled with so much love. "Amanda, honey, I'm so glad you're here."

Amanda turned to ice. It was as if a wall suddenly slid into place, separating her from her mom. "Let's keep this about the transplant. That's all I'm here for."

The tension in the room was thick, but the twin girls, though, they played happily with some blocks, totally clueless to their mom shooting daggers at her mom. It made things seem a little more normal.

"This is my girlfriend, V," Zack introduced me, and I offered a quick wave, not wanting to intrude on their intense family reunion.

Amanda nodded politely, her attention shifting to her children, who were now tugging at her sweater. "These are my twins, Cali and Casi, and my husband, David."

With the introductions out of the way, we found a seat in the stiff hospital chairs. I fidgeted with the hem of my shirt while Chloe and Amanda exchanged some awkward sentences about Amanda's health situation and the transplant procedure. It was obvious their relationship was strained, like a bridge that hadn't been crossed in years.

The conversation then turned to Zack and Amanda. "I can't believe how much you've grown," Amanda said to Zack, a spark of warmth in her eyes. "You were just a kid last time I saw you."

Zack nodded, eagerness in his voice. "Yeah, it's been a long time. I wish we could've stayed in touch."

The mention of their long separation seemed to hit a nerve. Amanda's expression hardened again. "Life happens. We all make choices."

Chloe tried to break through, "Amanda, I just want you to know I—"

"Chloe, please," Amanda stopped her, keeping it formal, like 'Mom' was a word too heavy to say. "Let's not do this now."

Chloe recoiled, biting her lip and looking at the floor. The room fell into an uncomfortable silence, broken only by the innocent giggles of Cali and Casi as they kept playing with their blocks.

The doctor entered then, breaking the tension. "We have the results. Zack, you are a match."

Relief and apprehension washed over Zack's face simultaneously. "I . . . I want to do this. For Amanda."

Amanda looked at Zack, her tough exterior softening. "Thank you, Zack. I know we haven't been part of each other's lives, but this . . . this means everything to me."

Chloe reached out, touching Amanda's hand, trying to bridge years in seconds. "Honey, I've missed you so much."

Amanda pulled her hand away gently, her voice soft but resolute. "I know you have, Chloe, um, uh, Mom. But we can't just pick up where we left off. There's a lot we need to sort out."

Zack, sensing the delicate nature of their reunion, shifted the focus. "We have time to figure this out. Right now, let's just take it one step at a time. Let's get through the transplant first."

Amanda nodded, gratitude in her eyes. "You're right. Thank you, Zack. Really."

Amanda stood to leave and the twins ran over to her, hugging her legs. She scooped them up, one in each arm, a smile breaking through her guarded exterior. She said her goodbyes and left with her husband and children.

Once the decision was made and Chloe signed off for a minor to be a donor, the surgery was scheduled and things moved quickly. Zack's transplant surgery was set in just two weeks. The doctor explained that, for the donor, the procedure was relatively straightforward. They would extract bone marrow from his pelvic bone using a specialized needle and syringe while he was under general anesthesia. The process would take between four to six hours, with an overnight hospital stay, maybe a couple of days stay, at the most. Zack's full recovery and return to his usual activities were expected within two weeks. The doctor reassured him that most donors only experience minimal pain and discomfort.

Curious, Zack asked, "Is it possible for anyone to be a bone marrow donor?"

The doctor shook his head gently. "Not exactly. The ideal bone marrow donor is typically between the ages of 18 and 35, and preferably a sibling of the patient. This increases the likelihood of a close tissue match. The key lies in the T-cells, these immune cells can attack any perceived foreign cells if the match isn't close enough. For bone marrow transplants, the most suitable donors are Match Related Donors, or MRDs, who share the same HLA tissue type as the patient. It's very fortunate for your sister, Zack. Only about a quarter of patients in need of a transplant have a fully matched sibling donor."

Chloe added, "That's why I couldn't be a donor, honey. I'm too old." Everyone laughed, adding a little levity to the tension.

Chloe thanked the doctor and walked out of the room. Following behind, Zack and I also left. He turned to me, his expression worried. "I'm doing the right thing, aren't I?"

I squeezed his hand, assuring him. "Yes, you are. You're giving your sister a chance at life. That's the most incredible gift anyone could give."

He nodded, a determined look in his eyes. "Then let's do this. For Amanda, for Cali and Casi, for our family."

Leaving the hospital, I felt hopeful. Despite the complexities of their family dynamics, today felt like a step toward something better for all of them.

ON THE WAY back from our meeting with Amanda, Chloe surprised me with an invitation to dinner. I think she hoped Zack would feel comfortable discussing the transplant surgery, especially with me there for support. Throughout dinner, the conversation occasionally steered toward the surgery, but Zack remained reserved, offering only brief comments.

After dinner, Chloe disappeared for a moment and returned with a box full of random stuff. Zack looked like he wanted to disappear. "Mom, seriously? Why are you dragging that stuff out here?"

Chloe was all smiles, rummaging through the box. "I was hunting for some more pictures of Amanda and found this box of your old trophies," she said, tossing me a look. "Hey, V, did you know Zack was the Tony Hawk of our town?"

Intrigued, I jumped off the couch to take a closer look. I picked up a gold trophy with a skateboarder dude on top. "Crash, Spring Roll champion 2013," I read out loud, impressed.

Zack joined me, shaking his head. "Nah, Ma, you got it wrong," he said, taking the trophy out of my hands. "Tony's too old. I was more like Ryan Sheckler."

"That's my boy," Chloe teased, "ever so humble."

Then a framed photo caught my eye. It was two kids, arm in arm. The caption read, "Mack & Zack, ride or die." I waved it at Chloe, my curiosity piqued. "Who's this?"

"That's Malia!" Chloe beamed.

"Malya—huh?" I did a double-take. The kid I pegged for a boy, thanks to the backward ball cap and loose threads, was actually a girl. Surprised, I blurted, "That's a girl?" A closer squint, and her softer edges came into focus.

"Yes, Ma-Leah," Chloe enunciated. "She was a total skater girl, always at the park. The boys were iffy at first, but she shredded hard and earned her stripes. Mack was her skater alias, and her and Zack? They were thick as thieves."

Zack, now fifty shades of red, said, "Mom, ancient history. Can we not?"

But I was already down the rabbit hole. "What's her story now?"

Chloe sighed, getting nostalgic. "Malia moved back to Hawaii with her family after seventh grade. We haven't seen them since then, but I stay in touch with her mom. They've always talked about moving back someday."

I raised an eyebrow, a teasing tone in my voice. "Did Zack have a thing for her?"

Zack shut that down fast, "No way! We were just skate pals. End of story."

I backed off, not wanting to make him more uncomfortable in front of his mom. But something told me there was more to Mack and Zack than met the eye.

6

UNRAVELING THE MYSTERY

The Prepped SAT class was in full swing Thursday night as I settled into my seat, ready for my first practice test. I hadn't even cracked open a study guide. Being there for Zack and his mom with Amanda's news, and accompanying them to the hospital, basically made me forget all about my study plans with Emma.

I sensed Emma's disappointment, even though she masked it with a smile. "It's okay, V," she had said. "Family first, right?"

Now, as Mr. Bennett announced, "You may open your tests and begin," a sense of dread washed over me. I tried to muster some self-reassurance. This was just the first of many practice tests. There was still plenty of time before the real thing in October. But it felt like a lousy pep talk.

The room was dead silent, everyone buried in their practice tests, when suddenly some idiot behind me totally biffed it and dropped his entire pencil case with a loud crash. I jumped, whipped around, and shot a glare at the guy two rows back. He just gave me this "my bad" shrug and dove right back into his test. But I stared a little too long and noticed he was just randomly shading in answers like he was playing 'eeny, meeny, miny, moe.' Kinda made me feel better, though. At least I wasn't the only one not ready for this test.

After the test was over, I spotted Jacob hanging around outside. *Since when does Jacob hang out at the library?* This was weird because he ghosted our study group tonight. Curiosity got the best of me, so I walked up to him. "Hey, Jacob, why'd you bail on the practice test?"

Before Jacob could even open his mouth, Mr. Pencil Case Disaster from earlier butted in, "Yo, haven't you heard? Jacob's like the SAT whisperer now. Dude scored a perfect 1600 a couple weeks back and peace'd out of our class faster than you can say 'dropout.' Guy's practically a legend."

I raised an eyebrow in disbelief. I couldn't help myself, saying, "Come on, you? 1600? As if."

Jacob rolled his eyes and was all, "Vi-o-let," dragging my name out like he was super annoyed, "believe it, girl. Now, how 'bout you stay in your lane?"

I just kinda backed away and shot Emma this "can you believe this?" look as we headed to the parking lot. Once we were in my car, I let it all out. "There's no way Jacob pulled off a perfect score without some serious shadiness. He's no Einstein if you know what I mean."

Emma just laughed it off. "Relax, V. Maybe he just got lucky with a tutor over the summer or something."

I shook my head, not buying it. "I don't think so; he totally cheated. I can feel it, like how I know this is gonna be my new mission. I'm gonna expose Jacob's SAT scam, just watch."

Emma sighed, like she was bracing herself for another one of my 'investigations.' "Oh great, V's on the case again. Another mystery to solve."

THE NEXT DAY, I was like a dog with a bone about this whole Jacob mystery. I literally couldn't stop thinking about it all morning. So, when lunchtime rolled around, I found Emma in the quad about to get in the food line. It was too crowded there so I pulled her over to a quieter spot in the shade of a nearby tree.

"Emma, I need to talk to you about Jacob," I began, my voice low.

"What about him?"

I got straight to the point. "This whole thing with the 'perfect score.' It's super fishy. I'm going full detective mode on this, starting today. I think I need to dig into Jacob's friends and—"

"You mean you're gonna spy on people?" Emma cut in. "Isn't that kinda . . . I don't know, sketchy? Besides, what if you're wrong?"

I leaned in, all serious. "But what if I'm right? I've gotta find out. And hey, I was hoping maybe you could help?"

Emma hesitated, biting her lip. "Look, V, you know I've got your back, always. But playing detective?" She paused, glancing away. "And after . . . you know—that whole kidnapping mess I got into freshman year, I swore off anything even close to danger. You remember me hiding in that driver's ed car last year, right?"

"Yeah, yeah, I get it," I said, giving her shoulder a reassuring squeeze. "I won't drag you into this. I'll fly solo."

She gave me a small, grateful smile. "Thanks, V. But please, be careful, okay? And keep me in the loop."

I nodded, already plotting my next move. First, I'd chat up some of Jacob's crew, and see if they'd spill any details about his study habits or if he'd been hanging with anyone new. I had to keep it low key though, throwing around cheating accusations was like playing with fire.

Something was up, though, I could feel it. This wasn't just about a test score. It was about playing fair and keeping it real. If Jacob was gaming the system, then someone needed to call him out. And that someone? Yeah, that's gonna be me.

By Saturday morning, the mystery of Jacob's perfect SAT score was still gnawing at me like a persistent itch. After enduring another session of the mind-numbingly dull Prepped class, I lingered behind, marshaling my courage to approach Mr. Bennett.

"Mr. Bennett?" I called out, catching him just as he was packing up his teaching arsenal.

He looked up, a face breaking into a friendly, if somewhat forgetful, smile. "Hey, it's V, right?" His attempt at remembering names was as half-hearted as his jokes.

I nodded, managing a polite smile.

"I'm not the greatest with names. Still learning everyone in the class. But you can call me Lucas. My dad is Mr. Bennett," he said with a laugh, trying for humor.

I smiled awkwardly, cutting to the chase. "It's about one of the students. Jacob. I heard he scored a perfect 1600 on his SATs."

Lucas arched an eyebrow, a flicker of interest crossing his face. "Jacob, huh? That's quite an achievement. What about it?"

Taking a deep breath, I dove in. "It's just that . . . his score seemed to come out of nowhere. I mean, is it common for someone to make such a drastic improvement? To jump from an average score to . . . *perfect*?"

He leaned against his desk, his demeanor shifting to one of thoughtful consideration. "Well, it is rare but not impossible. Some students have a breakthrough or find a study method that works really well for them. However, a jump to a perfect score is definitely unusual."

I nodded, feeling the gears in my mind turning faster. "Have you noticed anything off about Jacob? Like when he talked through our entire first session? Or his interactions with others?"

Lucas pondered for a moment, his brow furrowing. "He talked all through one of *my* classes? Are you sure? I thought Jacob was the quiet one who sat in the back. You know, he mostly kept to himself. But I did notice he became less engaged after our first session. Almost as if he didn't need the class anymore."

"That's just it, he didn't need the class anymore," I said, ignoring his comment about Jacob being 'the quiet one.' I continued, "He dropped your course when he got his perfect score."

Lucas's expression turned thoughtful. "That is interesting timing. But V, remember, correlation doesn't always mean causation. Do you think there's more to it?"

I sighed. "Actually, I do. And I'm going to find out what it is. It's just that, I feel like he's hiding something."

Lucas nodded slowly. "Well, if you're going to look into this, be careful not to jump to conclusions. And keep me updated, okay? If there's anything irregular, it's important for us to know."

"Thanks, Mr. Bennett. I mean, Lucas. I appreciate it." I said, feeling a sense of relief at having shared my concerns. But something still didn't sit right. How could he not remember that Jacob had been so disruptive during that first class? And why had he seemed so oblivious at the time? It was all adding to the enigma.

As I left the classroom, my mind was a hive of activity, buzzing with possibilities and theories. Jacob's sudden disinterest in the class, the timing of his score and his exit from the course—it all pointed to something more than just a stroke of good fortune. I knew I had to tread carefully, but I couldn't let this go. There was a mystery here, and I was determined to unravel it.

7

THE VIDEO

When I got home, the house seemed unusually quiet. I knew Dad and Scotty were at soccer but I didn't know where Mom was. Even though her car was in the driveway it didn't necessarily mean she was home. And, where was Lucky?

I was left alone with my thoughts, the conversation with Lucas still playing on a loop in my mind. I wanted to dig deeper into the mystery surrounding Jacob and his friends, but it was Saturday, and I would have to wait until Monday.

I heard the shower in Mom's bathroom turn on and relaxed a little. I kicked back on the couch and pulled out my phone. A familiar chime of a text message broke the silence, but it wasn't my phone. It was Mom's. She'd left it on the end table, next to the couch.

I knew I shouldn't pry, but curiosity overpowered me. I picked up her phone and saw a message from Mom's friend Rebecca.

Just saw the promo. It turned out great! The camera loves you! Here's the link.

Without a second thought, I clicked on the link attachment. The video that loaded was not what I expected. It was *my mom*, looking vibrant with makeup on, discussing her cancer journey. She spoke about her diagnosis, the surgeries, and how incredible the doctors at UCI (University of California-Irvine) were. Her words were inspiring, but they stung me with their newness.

"Hi, my name is Hannah Jiménez. I'm 41 years old and an English teacher of twenty years at Sierra High School in Orange. In September 2015, the day before my 39th birthday, I was given an awful diagnosis of Stage Four Breast Cancer. When I first got diagnosed, I had actually gone in to see my general practitioner because I felt a lump in my neck. I hadn't thought it was anything serious but since it hadn't gone away I thought I'd go in and get it checked. Eventually, I felt a lump in my breast and then I kind of knew.

"I have been through three different types of chemo, radiation, a double mastectomy, and another related surgery since then—but I'm still here. It's hard to explain the terrifying feeling you have when you're first given that diagnosis. I have two young kids. So at the time, your first thought is, 'Am I going to see my kids grow up?' Followed by, 'Am I going to be there for all the things I want to be there for?' And that's one of the hardest things. I have a 16-year-old daughter. . . . I wouldn't be sitting here right now if it weren't for UCI Medical Center. They've given me more time. I know I have a bad prognosis but every moment I've been able to spend with my husband, Carlos, and my two kids, and my family and my friends —It's just, it's a gift. Every single day."

I sat there, the glow of the screen from my mom's phone fading to black, my fingers frozen around it. Inside, a storm was brewing, a mess of emotions I couldn't quite name. Why hadn't she told me about the video? Weren't we past the whole 'secrets' phase? We were supposed to be a team, a united front, but there I was, feeling like the odd one out again.

Tears were threatening to spill over, blurring the edges of the room, but I wasn't about to give in to them. I was done being the clueless kid, shielded from the world's ugly truths. I wanted the unfiltered reality, no matter how much it stung.

The sound of the shower shutting off snapped me back to the present. Hastily, I placed Mom's phone back on the end table, wiping away the traitorous tears. I couldn't let her see me like this, raw and exposed.

When Mom came down the stairs, wrapped in that fluffy, forest green robe Dad had gotten her last Christmas, she looked relaxed, completely unaware of the chaos inside my head. "Hey, sweetie. Anything interesting happen while I was in the shower?"

I forced a smile, keeping my voice even. "Nope, just got home from my second Prepped class."

"Oh, how was it?" she asked, absent-mindedly.

"It was . . . fine," I replied, the word tasting like ash in my mouth. "We learned some hacks for memorizing vocabulary, formulas, and some rhyming strategies."

"Sounds intriguing," she said, but her eyes were distant, like she was somewhere else.

I couldn't hold back any longer. The words just tumbled out. "Oh, and Rebecca texted you. Your video is online."

Her face drained of color. "My video?"

"Yeah, the one where you talk about your cancer, your 'bad prognosis.' That one."

"V, sweetie, you're overreacting. It's just a hospital promo. It's nothing," she tried to downplay it.

But her words were like a slap. "Mom, I need the whole truth. No more pretending everything's normal. I have to know."

Our confrontation was cut short as the front door burst open. Scotty charged in with Lucky, his fur freshly trimmed, at his heels. "V! Look at Lucky's haircut! Funny, right?"

Mom and I locked eyes, an unspoken agreement passing between us. This wasn't the time or the place. I greeted Scotty and his goofy-looking dog with a smile, but inside, my mind was racing, spinning around the truth I still needed from Mom.

8

A DAY OF REMEMBRANCE

September 11th

The somber tone of the morning at Sierra High was set the moment Dr. Fitzgibbon's voice came over the intercom. His words, a tribute to those lost on 9/11, filled the hallways and classrooms with a respectful silence. I was only two months old when the attacks happened, but every year on this day since then has brought a wave of sadness and a reminder of a tragedy I had learned about through stories from my parents.

As the day progressed, the weight of the morning's remembrance lingered in the air. But I had a mission that required my focus. It was time to start unraveling the mystery surrounding Jacob's unrealistically perfect SAT score. Lunchtime provided the perfect opportunity.

I spotted one of Jacob's football buddies by his locker. I casually approached him, making sure Jacob was nowhere in sight. "Hey, can I ask you something?" I started, feigning a casual curiosity. "I heard Jacob aced his SATs. Did he share any study tips with you guys?"

The football player, caught off guard, just shrugged. "Nah, Jacob does his own thing. But he's always been smart, ya know?"

I nodded, moving on to find another one of Jacob's friends. This time, I caught Kevin in the hallway. We'd had geometry together freshman year and I remembered he hung out with Jacob during class. "Hey, Kevin, I'm trying to up my SAT score. Jacob did really well, right? Did he use any special prep books or anything?"

Kevin was a bit more talkative, but not helpful. "Oh, Jacob? Yeah, he killed it. But no idea how, honestly. We don't really talk about that stuff."

The guarded answers weren't giving me much, but it was clear Jacob's friends were protective of him. I needed someone less cautious, someone who might slip up.

Finally, near the end of lunch, I found one of Jacob's less discreet friends alone. "Hey, you're in my Prepped class, right? I'm trying to figure out how to boost my SAT score. Got any tips for me?"

He laughed. "You and me both, V. You should ask Jacob. Man, he's got some tricks up his sleeve, for sure. We don't know much, but he's always been ahead of the game. We heard he found some sort of loophole or something."

"We?"

"Me and the other guys in the class. We all want to score high, too, but so far, Jacob's not talking. Want me to let you know if I find out anything?"

"Yes, that would be lifesaving, thank you! My parents will kill me if I don't do well on the test. But I barely have time to study these days. You know how it is, right?"

"Totally. I hear ya," he said as the bell rang. "Well, I gotta go. See you in class."

"Totally," I replied, waving. *Totally?* I cringed as I turned to leave. Acting cool was not a good look on me. But I did get a new lead. Now to figure out what this 'loophole' was. My mind raced with possibilities. What kind of loopholes were there? And more importantly, how many other people were involved?

I knew I was onto something, I just didn't know what. So far, this investigation was turning up more questions than answers. But one thing was clear: there was definitely more to this story, and I was determined to uncover it.

9
JUGGLING ACT

J uggling school, my suspicions about Jacob, SAT studies, and my concern for my mom *and* my boyfriend had become my new normal. Zack's upcoming transplant surgery was only a week away, and he hadn't mentioned it since the day we met Amanda last week.

So, after another long day of school, I decided to surprise Zack. Maybe an impromptu date would lighten the mood. I texted him.

> Hey, you don't have to work today, right?

His reply came almost immediately.

ZACK

> Nah, a couple guys asked for more hours last night so I gave them my shifts for the rest of the week. Not feeling much like working these days. Why? What's up?

Nothing. Thought maybe we could hang out.
May I buy you a Boba tea? I need a Zack-fix.

Sure, sounds good. Meet you at our spot?

See you there, Zackybear!

'Our spot' was a quaint little café near school, a frequent favorite. As I walked in, I spotted Zack at our usual table by the window. Two drinks already in front of him. His smile was warm but didn't quite reach his eyes.

"Hey, this was supposed to be my treat, remember?" I gave him a quick kiss on the cheek, sliding into the seat across from him.

"I wanted a coffee instead; haven't been sleeping great lately."

I sighed, knowing better than to bring up the surgery. We sipped our drinks as we talked about everything and nothing, completely avoiding the subject.

"Hey, you're going to ace the next practice test," Zack said, trying to sound encouraging.

I smiled weakly, "I'll try. But right now, I'm more worried about you." Unable to ignore it any longer, I plunged in. "Are you okay?"

Zack took a long drink from his coffee, his gaze fixed on the cup. "Yeah, I'm fine. Just a lot on my mind, you know?"

I reached across the table, placing my hand over his. "Talk to me, Zack. You haven't mentioned the surgery all week. I can't imagine how scared you must be right now."

He slowly pulled his hand away, looking out the window. "I don't know, V. It's a lot. I just need some time to myself, to process everything."

I felt a pang of concern but respected his need for space.

"Okay, I get it. We don't have to talk about it now. I have to study with Emma tonight, anyway."

Zack gave a grateful smile. "Thanks, V. I appreciate it."

We left the café and I watched him walk toward his car, shoulders hunched, grappling with the weight of the unknown.

I pulled out my phone and texted Emma.

> Hey, up for studying after dinner? Need to cram for the next practice test and clear my head.

She replied in an instant.

EMMA

> Absolutely! I'll bring my notes. Meet you at the library!

As I drove home, my thoughts were a jumble of worry for Zack and finding proof that Jacob cheated. Focusing on studying with Emma was what I needed right now, especially if I hoped to get a decent score on my own SAT efforts. I needed to give Zack the space he asked for and keep my mind occupied. I had to find that delicate balance—supporting Zack and dealing with my own tangled emotions. It was a balancing act, and I was learning to walk the tightrope.

EMMA MET me at the library so we'd have some peace and quiet. Though they meant well, my mom would want to chat with Emma, and Emma's grandma would want to distract me with food and snacks. The library was a quiet reprieve, but my mind was far from quiet. It was a whirlwind of formulas, vocabulary,

Jacob, Zack, and Mom. A wonder I could think at all. Emma had planned an intense study session for us. Her notes were next-level organized, complete with color coding. But I just couldn't get it together to focus on studying.

"Okay, V, let's start with math," she said, spreading her notes on the table. Her voice pulled me back to the present.

"Right, math," I muttered, trying to concentrate. Emma went through a complex algebra problem, but my thoughts kept drifting back to Zack. Was he feeling anxious about the surgery? Should I have pushed him to talk more?

"V, are you even listening?" Emma's question snapped me back to reality.

"Sorry, Emma. Just . . . a lot on my mind," I apologized, shaking my head to clear it.

She gave me a sympathetic look. "I know you're worried about Zack. But he wanted some space, remember? Let's focus on this. It'll help distract you."

She was right. I needed to compartmentalize my worries and get my brain into the proper headspace. For the next hour, as we dove into practice questions, Emma's explanations began to penetrate my fog of distractions. The formulas and equations finally made sense.

As we switched to the verbal section, my phone buzzed. It was Zack:

Thinking of you. Hope studying's going well .

I smiled. He was thinking of me, even with everything he was going through.

Thanks, Zee. Means a lot. Hope you're OK 

I texted back before turning off my phone. It was time to focus.

The library's quiet hum and the rustle of pages turning provided a soothing backdrop as Emma and I reviewed vocabulary and reading comprehension strategies. She quizzed me, her questions becoming increasingly challenging, pushing me to think harder.

At last, I felt a sense of preparedness I hadn't felt earlier. "Thanks, Emma. I needed this."

She packed her notes, smiling. "Anytime, V. You're going to do great on the practice test. And remember, it's just that—practice."

Driving home, I felt more in control. The second guesses that had clouded my day were slowly fading, replaced by a quiet confidence. Deciding to tackle each thing one at a time, I was ready for whatever came next.

IO

BUYING IN

The rest of the week seemed to drag on endlessly, each day blending into the next. Emma and I studied every chance we got, her methodical approach a lifeline in a sea of algebraic formulas and daunting vocabulary words. Surrounded by prep books and practice tests, we quizzed each other, dissected tricky math problems, and parsed dense reading passages. The intensity of our study sessions was both exhausting and exhilarating. She had a knack for breaking it down for me, making the insurmountable suddenly manageable.

By Thursday night, we were ready. I took the second practice test, feeling more confident with each answered question. When I finished and tallied my score, I let out a silent cheer. My score had jumped significantly. Emma's encouragement and our joint study efforts had paid off.

Now that I was more confident with a good practice score, my detective instincts were back in full swing and I was armed and ready for Saturday's Prepped class.

Friday after school, Zack surprised me with an afternoon at

the park. We hadn't spent much time together all week since he'd asked for space and I needed to focus on studying with Emma. So when I got his text, it was a nice surprise.

We met at our favorite bench, a fun place for people watching and getting lost in the crowd. Once we settled down, side by side, Zack reached for my hand and asked, "How goes the studying with Emma?"

"Actually great! She's really good at breaking everything down for me. We both did well on last night's practice test. But we don't need to talk about that right now. How are you doing?" I gave his hand a light squeeze.

He turned to me, a wistful smile on his lips. "Just thinking. About the surgery, about everything. It's a lot to process, you know?"

I nodded, understanding all too well. "It's okay to be scared. It's a big deal."

He let out a deep breath, his eyes meeting mine. "I am scared. Like, what if something goes wrong? What if—"

I cut him off gently. "Hey, don't spiral down that path. You're strong, and you've got a great team of doctors. Plus, you've got me. I'm not going anywhere."

Zack's smile deepened, a glimmer of his usual self shining through. "I know. And that means everything to me. You being here . . ." His voice trailed off.

We sat in silence for a while, watching as the sun began to dip lower in the sky, casting a golden hue over the park. Eventually, Zack spoke up again, "I want you to know, V, no matter what happens, I'm grateful. For you, for everything."

My heart swelled with emotion. "Zack, I love you. We're in this together, okay? Every step of the way."

He nodded, his expression vulnerable. As we stood up to leave, I felt a sense of determination settle over me. I was committed to Zack, to supporting him through whatever lay ahead.

He walked me to my car in silence, each of us lost in our own thoughts, but our joined hands spoke volumes. This was the calm before the storm, a precious moment of peace before the gigantic hurricane awaiting us. I would be there for Zack through the storm and beyond, my devotion resolute.

THE NEXT MORNING, while Lucas shared more test-taking tips and strategies, I surveyed the room. A group of guys, all in Jacob's circle, sat together at the back of class.

When class ended, the same group huddled outside the library, whispering in hushed tones. I lingered nearby, pretending to rummage through my backpack. Snatches of their conversation floated over to me. "I'm thinking of buying in…" one of them said. "Jacob says it's a sure thing…" another whispered.

'Buying in?' The phrase echoed in my mind. Were they talking about paying Jacob? For what? Cheating on their SATs seemed like the only logical conclusion, but how was he pulling it off? The tests were randomized, making it impossible to predict the questions.

I strained to hear more, but their voices dropped further, their words lost in a mumble. Frustrated, I zipped up my backpack and walked over to Emma. The pieces of the puzzle were there, but they weren't quite fitting together yet.

Once we were in the parking lot, out of earshot, I told her what I'd overheard.

"But how can Jacob guarantee a 'sure thing'?" Emma asked.

"Maybe he's selling test answers?" I guessed. "But I don't see how that could be possible. I mean, it's ludicrous. No one knows which test questions will be administered on any given test day. It's just that the guys seemed so convinced."

"I don't get it. He's gotta have some kind of angle."

"Yeah, I'm sure he does. But I need more than a hunch; I need concrete proof."

"Good luck with that," Emma said, adding, "but, be careful, okay? You don't know what Jacob's capable of."

"I know. But I have to keep a closer eye on Jacob and his friends if I'm going to crack this. Don't worry, I'll be careful."

II

MENACING MESSAGE

onday.

New week, new threat in my ongoing saga. As I swung open my locker, a piece of notebook paper, torn and crumpled, took a nosedive to the floor. Bending down, I snatched it up, my eyes immediately locking onto the bold, black Sharpie letters scrawled across in a desperate ALL CAPS.

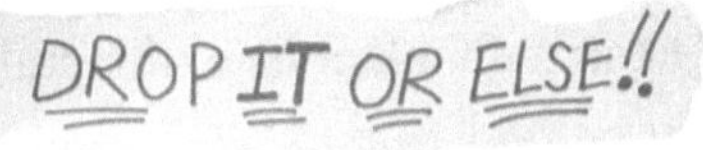

A chill zipped down my spine—not from fear, but from the thrill of the chase. Signature? None. But it didn't take a detective to guess this was Jacob's handiwork. Word gets around when you start poking in dark corners.

Instead of backing down, I felt a surge of defiance. Jacob, with his cryptic threats, was playing a game he didn't know I excelled at. I shoved the note into my bag—a piece of evidence in the increasingly murky puzzle.

The rest of the morning, I was there in body but not in spirit, my mind racing with the implications of the note. Lunch couldn't come soon enough. Emma was my first stop.

"Emma, check out the welcome gift I got this morning," I said, sliding the note across the table to her.

Her eyes scanned it, widening slightly. "V, this is serious. Do you think it's from Jacob?"

"Who else? He's caught wind I'm onto him. This just adds another layer to the mystery." I reclaimed the note and buried it deep in my bag, just before Zack showed up.

"But it's a threat, V," Emma's voice was laced with concern. "Shouldn't you tell someone? At least tell Zack. What if Jacob tries something?"

I shook my head, a plan forming. "No way I'm backing down. And Zack's got enough on his plate with his surgery tomorrow. This high school drama can wait."

Emma gave a reluctant nod. "Just be careful, okay?"

"Always am," I said with a wink, just as Zack joined us, tray loaded like it was his last meal.

"What's up?" he asked, oblivious to the undercurrents.

Emma quickly shifted gears. "Well, nothing's wrong with your appetite," she teased, taking the focus off me.

"Thank you," I mouthed to her.

She gave me a slight nod and continued, "Eating for an army, Zack? Man, I wish I had your metabolism."

"What are you talking about, Emma? I've seen you carb load before a big soccer game. Heck, you eat pizza and spaghetti like they're your last meal."

"Do not!" she protested in mock indignation.

"Okay, you two. Break it up," I said, laughing.

Even though I was laughing on the outside, my insides felt like butterflies swirling around in a frenzy. As the lunch bell rang, sending us back to class, I couldn't shake the feeling of being watched. I kept a wary eye out for Jacob and his crew. His desperate note might have raised the stakes, but it also confirmed I was on the right track. There was something he was desperate to hide, and I was more determined than ever to drag it into the light.

★ ★ ★ ★ ★

AFTER SCHOOL, I stopped at Zack's place to keep him company. He played it cool at school, but I knew how scared he was. His transplant surgery was scheduled early the next morning.

I let myself in and found him on the couch, lost in the mindless world of channel surfing. "Hey, babe," he said, without taking his eyes off the TV.

"Hey," I replied, sliding onto the couch and planting a quick kiss on his lips. "So, how's the bravest guy I know doing?"

He killed the TV and turned to face me, a storm brewing in his eyes. "I've been doing some thinking, you know, about the surgery, life, the whole nine yards."

I grabbed his hand, giving it a reassuring squeeze. "Zack, you don't have to play the hero with me. It's okay to admit it's freaking you out."

He shook his head, a half-smile playing on his lips. "It's not about fear. It's about stepping up. For Amanda, my family." He took a deep breath. "This is my shot to make a difference, to be part of something bigger. Scary? Sure. But it's the right play."

Listening to him, I saw him in a new light. Zack, in that

moment, was showing the kind of guts that'd put most adults to shame.

"I get the risks," he went on, a firmness in his voice. "But if this gives Amanda a fighting chance, then it's game on. Whatever happens to me."

I felt a lump in my throat but shoved it down. No way was I going to fall apart on him. "You're something else, Zack. I don't know how you do it."

He shrugged, that humble, Zack way of his. "I just focus on what matters. And hey, I couldn't face any of this without you, V. You're my anchor in this crazy storm."

He pulled me into a tight hug. It was one of those hugs that said a thousand words—a promise, a comfort, a sharing of strength.

I knew whatever tomorrow threw at us, Zack's courage and heart would carry him through. He was more than just a patient or a brother; he was a living, breathing lesson in courage. Being by his side, part of his story, felt like a privilege.

We spent the rest of the evening just being there, together. Talking, laughing, sometimes just sitting. It was the calm before the storm, and in those quiet moments, I saw Zack for who he really was—a rock in the chaos, a steady pulse of calm in the madness. And for that, I loved him all the more.

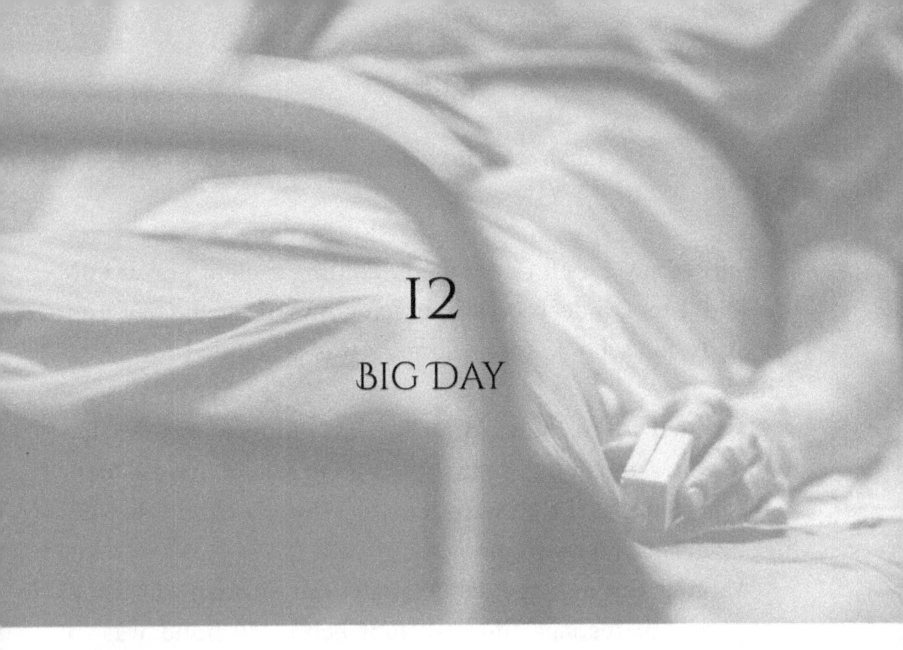

12
BIG DAY

uesday.

In the dead of night, I was wide awake, my mind replaying the last two weeks like a 'whodunit' film stuck on loop. Zack's bravery, his commitment to his sister, our late-night talks—it all led to today. My eyes flicked to the clock. 5:02 a.m. I figured I might as well start the day.

Sitting on the edge of my bed, I stretched, making a mental pact to channel a bit of Zack's bravery. His selfless act was a guiding light in the murky waters of my thoughts.

I grabbed my phone, shooting a text to Zack, knowing he was already on his way to the hospital.

> Good luck today. I'll be there as soon as I can. I love you.

His response was quick.

> Thanks. I'll see ya on the other side 🫶

A lump formed in my throat as I typed back,

You're going to be amazing. I'm here for you, always 🤍

I closed my eyes for a moment, sending a silent prayer into the void. I took a deep breath, bracing myself for the day, and got ready for school. Zack's surgery was scheduled for seven o'clock.

I wanted to be there, to be his last glimpse of normalcy before going under, but he insisted I go to school, have a "normal" day. Sure, as if that were possible. But his mom was with him, so at least he wasn't alone.

Walking through the school halls felt surreal, the usual cacophony of teenage life a distant echo. My mind was in that hospital, wondering how Zack and Amanda were holding up.

Focus was a foreign concept in class. My leg jittered non-stop, my pencil drumming a relentless beat. The lunch bell was a sweet escape.

Emma found me at my locker. "Hey, how are you holding up?" she asked, her eyes etched with worry.

I shrugged, my voice a faint whisper. "It's happening now. He's in surgery."

"Shouldn't it be over by now? I thought it only took four hours?"

"They delayed it. His surgeon was caught up in another emergency. His mom texted me. She said they just wheeled him in about twenty minutes ago."

"It's going to be okay, V. Zack's strong, and so are you." Emma's hug was a small island of comfort.

I nodded, clinging to her words. "I just wish I could be there."

The rest of the day was a blur, my phone agonizingly silent.

The wait was excruciating, a test of endurance I wasn't sure I could pass.

School finally ended, and I rushed to the hospital. Being in that waiting room felt like the closest I could get to Zack.

Time dragged on, every minute an eternity. Then, my phone buzzed, a message from Chloe:

> Surgery went well. They're both in recovery now. Will update soon.

Relief washed over me like a tidal wave. I quickly replied,

> I'm so glad! Thank you for telling me. I'm here —in the waiting room.

Gratitude and exhaustion swept through me. They had made it through the toughest part. The first hurdle was cleared.

I leaned back and closed my eyes, a silent thank you escaping my lips.

★ ★ ★ ★ ★

IN THE STERILE quiet of the hospital room, Chloe and I took turns keeping a watchful eye over Zack. It was like some kind of grim relay race where no one wanted to drop the baton. During my shift, I sat beside him, his hand in mine, my thumb absent-mindedly tracing circles on his skin.

Chloe came back, armed with two cups of iced tea, a small gesture of normalcy in an otherwise abnormal situation. She handed me one, collapsing into the chair at the foot of Zack's bed. I mouthed a silent "thank you," taking a sip, my eyes never leaving Zack's unnaturally pale face. "He looks so pale," I whispered, more to myself than to her.

Chloe let out a light chuckle, breaking the room's somber mood. "Oh, honey, this is Zack we're talking about. When he was born, he was practically translucent. He was this tiny preemie, and it took forever for him to get any color. I think all his melanin was on backorder or something." Her voice trailed off, lost in the memory, shaking her head with a wistful smile.

"But boy did he turn heads whenever we went out," Chloe continued a minute later. "There was this one time, let's see, Zackery would have been about two. By then, he had a head full of bouncy, spiral curls, and with those blue-green eyes and long lashes, well, people often mistook him for a girl. It didn't matter what he wore either. I coulda dressed him from head-to-toe in blue-jean overalls and T-shirts with tiny footballs on them, and sure enough someone, somewhere, always had to come up and tell me what a cute little girl he was.

"Anyway, on this day in particular, I was in a bad mood. I don't recall why, but I know I was. I'd had to bring the kids with me to the market and I was in a hurry. Amanda must have been eleven or twelve, and she didn't like going to the market with me, so she hung back and sort of trailed after us at a distance. I'd put Zackery in that little seat up in front of the shopping cart and headed down the produce aisle. As I put a head of lettuce into the cart, an elderly woman, with skin as white as snow and the hair to match, walked right up to me and said, 'Oh my, what gorgeous curls that little girl has. And goodness, what beautiful blue eyes. She is simply an angel! You must just love being her **nanny**.' To which I replied, through clenched teeth, 'I'm *his mother. My son* came out of *my* vagina!' Poor Amanda kept on walking, pretending she didn't know me. The lady looked at Amanda, then at Zack, then back at me. She turned even whiter, like a ghost. Then, without a word, she snapped her gaping mouth shut, did an about face, and scurried away."

Zack stirred and mumbled something, his eyes fluttering open.

"Hey there, sleepyhead," Chloe said, her voice a mix of relief and warmth. She squeezed his hand gently. "What did you say, sweetheart?"

I stood and moved to his other side, needing to be closer.

"I said," Zack's voice was barely above a rasp, "are you still telling that embarrassing story, Mom?"

Chloe's laughter broke the heaviness in the room. "Heard that, did you?"

"Please stop telling it," Zack groaned, a hint of playfulness under his complaint. "It's the worst."

"Why? Can't handle the fact that you came out of my womb?" Chloe teased, her humor a sharp contrast to the seriousness of her previous story.

Zack made a face, half-smiling. "No, it's not that. It's just . . . that that lady thought I was a *girl!*"

Our laughter lightened the mood, a brief respite from the hospital's oppressive atmosphere. I leaned in, asking softly, "How are you feeling?"

"My throat's dry, but I'm okay," he managed, his smile weak but genuine.

Chloe smoothed his hair back, maternal and tender. "The doctors said the surgery went well. You did great, honey."

Zack's gaze flitted between us. "And Amanda? How's she doing?"

Chloe's face lit up. "She woke up before you. Worried sick about her little brother. She wanted me to be here when you woke up. She's doing well, all thanks to you."

"She always was quicker than me," Zack smirked. "But what did the docs say?"

"They're optimistic. It's early days yet, you've given her an incredible gift, son. We're all proud of you."

Zack's eyes were heavy, but he pushed on. "Where is she? I want to see her."

"She's with her family," Chloe said, her voice thick with emotion. "They're beyond grateful, Zack. But you need to rest now. You can see her soon."

"You've been so brave," I told him, squeezing his hand as if I could convey everything I felt in that simple gesture.

Zack's voice faded to a whisper. "It's weird, ya know. I barely know her, and yet . . ."

Chloe took his hand, tears in her eyes. "You gave your sister a second chance, Zack. That's what family does."

He nodded slowly, absorbing her words, and then drifted off, his sleep peaceful, the kind that comes after facing your biggest fears and coming out the other side.

13

A DELICATE BALANCE

A few hours later, doctor's green light in hand, I gently maneuvered Zack's wheelchair through the hospital's sterile maze. He was slumped back, his eyelids drooping, just a shadow of his usual self. A nurse with empathetic eyes told me his weakness was par for the course post-bone marrow donation. But knowing that didn't make it any easier to see him like this.

As we rolled up to Amanda's room, the gravity of what Zack had done hit me. The halls were eerily quiet, the distant beeps of machines and my own footsteps the only soundtrack. Right outside her room, Zack lifted his head, his eyes showing a flicker of the old Zack. "I need to do this alone," he murmured, his voice barely there.

I gave him a nod, got the unspoken message, and wheeled him inside. As I eased the door almost closed, leaving just a crack, Zack's voice, faint but sure, filled the room. "Hey, Mads, did I give you enough superpowers to beat this thing?"

Her laughter came through clear, a sound that seemed too big for that small room. "Zacky, my sweet Zacky. Get over here, little brother, and let me hug you!" Her voice was stronger than his but not without its own fragility.

Standing in the hallway, their reunion was like a melody—laughter, soft rustles, murmurs of conversation I couldn't hear but felt in my bones. It was the sound of a bond being rebuilt, of healing and rediscovery.

Twenty minutes later, my phone buzzed with Zack's text:

> Hey, you should head home. I'm gonna hang here with Mads. The nurse will take me back later. Thanks for today. You're the best 😊

Walking to my car, the hospital lights dimming in the distance, I felt this deep, satisfying exhaustion. It had been a day of highs and lows, emotional roller coasters. My body was spent, but my spirit? It was soaring. Watching Zack and Amanda reconnect, seeing years of distance fade in moments, it was something special.

The stars seemed to shine a bit brighter that night, mirroring the light of human connection that had just grown stronger. It hit me then—sometimes the most profound acts of love aren't loud or showy. They're in the quiet sacrifices, the kind made for family, for newfound ties. And that's exactly what Zack had done.

THE LUNCH BELL at school had become my new signal, not for grabbing a bite, but for a mission of a different kind. With Zack laid up in the hospital, I'd taken on the role of his personal homework courier. No way was I going to let his grades tank while he was out.

First up was his AP Lit class, taught by none other than my mom. I was about to barge into her classroom, expecting to find her deep in teacher talk with Miss Tisdale, her co-teacher, when I caught a snippet of their conversation. It was enough to freeze me in my tracks.

"When I die . . ." That was my mom's voice, eerily calm. A chill raced down my spine.

"But you're not dying! Are you?" Miss Tisdale's voice was a mix of panic and disbelief. "You can't . . . you're not going to die, right?"

Mom's reply had this philosophical edge to it. "Of course I am. We all are, eventually. I just happen to know what's going to kill me."

I couldn't just stand there. Bursting into the room, my voice was filled with fear and desperation. "Mom! What do you mean you know what's going to kill you?"

She turned, her face a blend of regret and motherly worry. "Oh, honey, I didn't want you to hear that."

"Well, I did. So what does it mean?" I demanded, my heart hammering in my chest.

She let out a heavy sigh, the kind that carried a ton of weight. "It means that, realistically, cancer is probably what will end my life. But, sweetie, that could be years down the road."

"How many years are we talking?" My voice was a shaky whisper, grappling with the reality of it all. "Do you have twenty years? Ten? Will you be there for my college graduation, my wedding?"

Her hands enveloped mine, warm and reassuring. "I don't have all the answers, sweetie. But I'm fighting. I plan to stick around for as much as I can."

Her words, meant to be comforting, just hammered home

the inevitable. I nodded, a silent acknowledgment of the new, brutal truth we were facing.

The room fell into a heavy silence, the kind that's loaded with things left unsaid and tears held back. Miss Tisdale, maybe sensing the need for a break in the tension, spoke up. "It's good to see you, V. What brings you here today?"

It was like she threw me a lifeline, pulling me back from the edge. "Oh, right," I remembered why I was there in the first place, a task that now seemed so minor. "I'm here for Zack's homework."

"Of course, I'll get that for you right now," Miss Tisdale said, shifting into professional mode, maybe trying to bring back a sense of normalcy. She started gathering Zack's assignments, the rustling of papers a weirdly comforting sound.

Mom and I shared a look, an entire conversation without words. We both stared at the floor, perhaps trying to find some peace in the little distraction.

Waiting for Zack's homework, I found myself caught between the mundane routine of school life and the heavy realities we were dealing with. It was a tightrope walk between everyday normal and the profound truths of life.

14

THINKING OF YOU

Zack's road to recovery was turning out smoother than I'd dared to hope. After only two nights in the hospital, his mom brought him home by Thursday afternoon. I couldn't wait to see him. All day at school, my mind was a runaway train of anticipation, each second stretching out longer than the last.

As soon as the final bell cut through the air, I was out the door, making a beeline for Zack's place. My heart did a jittery dance of excitement. Despite his texts assuring me he was doing okay, I needed to see him, to lay my own eyes on him.

I reached his door, knocked lightly, and held my breath. The door creaked open, and there was Zack. Tiredness was etched on his face, but his smile was like a beam of sunlight cutting through the fog.

"Hey, V," he greeted me, stepping aside to let me in.

"Hey!" I stepped inside, my eyes sweeping the place. "Is your mom here?"

"She just stepped out to run some errands and to check on Amanda," he said, shuffling to the living room in his sweats and oversized T-shirt. "She figured you'd be my keeper for the day." He winked, and that familiar thrill zipped through me.

"Your keeper, huh?" I giggled, feeling a surge of excitement. "I brought popcorn and a stack of movies. How are you really feeling?"

His reply was pure Zack charm. "A whole lot better now you're here."

A felt a flush of warmth as I glanced at our movie choices. "Action or comedy tonight?"

"You can stay that long? What about your practice test?"

"It's postponed. Our instructor had something come up. Next one's not till next Thursday, and the last practice test the Tuesday after that. So tonight, I'm all yours."

"Perfect." His grin was contagious as he patted a pillow fortress on the couch.

"So, which movie?" I said, still standing over him.

"You pick."

We settled in, the popcorn's aroma mingling with Zack's familiar scent. I picked a movie and dimmed the lights, the room wrapping around us in a comforting embrace. Zack seemed at ease, but I could feel the residue of his ordeal in the slight tension of his body.

"If you need a break or anything, just say so, okay?" I offered, concerned.

His hand found mine, a grounding touch. "I'm good. Really. Just being here with you is the best kind of recovery."

The movie played on, but it was just background noise to our shared bubble of contentment. At some point, Zack's head rested on my shoulder, his steady breathing a rhythm reassuring melody.

Relief washed over me. He was safe, right here with me, and for now, that was all that mattered.

We laughed, talked, and simply basked in each other's presence. It was one of those nights where the simplest moments felt like magic, a reminder of how extraordinary the ordinary can be when you're with the right person.

ON FRIDAY, Chloe and Zack's doctor gave us the go-ahead for a beach trip, with a strict "no heroics" policy. The idea of a sunset beach picnic had a perfect blend of romance and chill vibes. I packed up a blanket, a cooler with our favorite snacks, and a couple of beach chairs, the excitement bubbling inside me for a quiet evening by the sea with Zack.

The beach welcomed us with open arms, the waves singing a soothing tune. We spread out on the soft sand, diving into our feast of assorted meats, cheeses, crackers, and fruit, each bite tasting like a slice of the serene scene around us. Zack was all about the small joys, his time in the hospital giving him a new appreciation for the little things.

With my heart doing nervous gymnastics, I decided it was time. I wanted to share the poem I'd written for him, my heart poured out in words. Popping a grape into my mouth for a little courage boost, I cleared my throat and began, "I wrote you something last night. I couldn't focus on studying for my APUSH test, you were all I could think about. I call it 'Thinking of You.' Here it goes..."

My voice was a bit shaky at first, but I found my rhythm,, the words weaving a delicate dance of longing and love.

Who am I kidding?
How can I study when
All I think about is
The feeling of your lips
On my lips

How can I study when
I close my eyes
And see your smiling face
Your arms reaching for my embrace

I love the feeling of
Your hand in mine
The way you look at me
Like it's just us
Lost in time

I love your touch
The magic of your kiss
Melting away my nerves
Flipping that switch
It is beyond bliss

Finishing, I looked up to see Zack's eyes, deep like the ocean, reflecting a sea of emotions.

"Wow, V. That's . . . that's beautiful," he said, his voice wrapping around me. "Come here, babe." His arms were an inviting haven as we lay back, watching the sky dress up in orange, pink, and lavender hues.

The sunset faded into twilight, and Zack's kiss under the first stars was like the perfect endnote to our day. His kiss was a promise, a whisper of dreams yet to come.

We pulled away, and he looked at me with a contented smile. "What am I missing?"

I blinked, confused. "What do you mean?"

He stretched out, his toes teasing the cool sand. His gaze at the starry expanse above was thoughtful. "I mean, here I am, having saved my sister, watching a killer sunset, kissing the most amazing girl. How does it get any better than this? What's missing?" He paused, then grinned. "Ah, tacos!"

His out-of-the-blue taco craving cracked me up. "We just ate! You're impossible," I said, playfully shoving his shoulder.

His laugh blended with the sound of the waves, a perfect harmony. "Tacos always make things better."

Sitting there, sand cooling beneath us, the endless ocean stretching out, I realized these were the moments that made life worth living. It was the laughter, the love, the simple things. And yeah, tacos did sound pretty great right then.

15
PREPARED FOR PREPPED

The fourth Prepped class was in full swing Saturday morning, and I found myself more observant than ever. After my initial embarrassment over the first practice test fail, I managed to bump up my score to a solid 1360 on the second test. Perhaps not Ivy League material, but a decent improvement for me.

Lucas was at the front, talking about the importance of aiming high. "For schools like Harvard, you're looking at needing a 1540 at least," he said, his voice echoing in the classroom.

I glanced around the room, my thoughts drifting. Harvard? That was a universe away from my aspirations. But still, I couldn't help but wonder about the others in the class. How realistic was a 1540 for most of us here?

I scanned the room, stopping at the group of guys who all seemed to know Jacob. They were mostly jocks, the kind of guys who spent more time on the field than with their noses in a book. I found their sudden interest in academic excellence quite strange. Was it a coincidence all of them knew Jacob? Especially since some of them didn't even go to our school?

These thoughts plagued me as Lucas continued, "Next week is our last class before the official test. Make sure you're prepared."

Two more practice tests and one more class before October 7th. I needed to keep my eyes and ears open. Where it concerned Jacob, nothing about this felt right.

As class ended, I watched Jacob's crew closely. They were laughing, slapping each other's backs. They seemed confident —too confident? Did they know something the rest of us didn't?

As students filed out, I lingered, pretending to organize my notes. I overheard bits and pieces of their conversation. "...can't believe how easy it was..." one of them said. "...just follow the plan..." another voice chimed in.

My heart raced. They were definitely up to something. Were they cheating? And if so, how were they planning to pull it off on test day? My mind buzzed with questions and theories.

Emma was waiting for me outside. "Did you hear any of that?" I asked, my voice low.

She shook her head. "No, what's going on?"

I quickly filled her in. "I think Jacob's buddies have some sort of scheme for the SATs planned. They're too confident, and it's not just arrogance. We need to find out what they're planning."

Emma's eyes widened. "But how? We can't just accuse them without proof."

"I know," I said, my mind working overtime. "We need to be smart about this. Observe, listen. Maybe we can catch them slipping up, revealing their plan."

As we walked out to the parking lot, I felt discouragement and frustration. This was about so much more than just a test; it was a matter of integrity. I had to uncover the truth.

16

ECHOES OF FAREWELL

That afternoon, I found myself in the hospital again. This time, I was visiting Amanda with Zack. I could feel his tension—worry and hope—as he lightly knocked on her hospital room's door.

"Come in," came a cheerful voice from inside.

We entered to find Amanda sitting up in bed, her face brighter than I had expected. "Zack! And hello again, V," she said with a warm smile.

"Hey, Amanda," Zack greeted, a relieved grin spreading across his face. "How are you feeling?"

"Much better than I look," Amanda joked, adjusting her pillows. "Sit, sit! Tell me about the outside world. I'm living vicariously through you guys now."

Our conversation meandered through the most ordinary of topics, yet each word seemed to defy the sterile, whitewashed walls of the hospital room. School gossip, stories about our friends, and even a playful debate about which was better— relentless rain or scorching sun. Each topic seemed a small rebellion against the clinical setting we were in.

Amanda's untamed laughter filled the room, challenging the hum of medical equipment. Her eyes sparkled with a mischief that belied the gravity of her situation. In these moments, her unyielding spirit transformed our surroundings. The hospital bed, with its crisp, impersonal sheets, became just another spot for a friendly chat; the IV stand beside her, an inconsequential detail in the background of our shared laughter.

It was almost easy to forget, amid the warmth of our conversation, the severity of the battle she was quietly waging. Her laughter was a vibrant reminder of perseverance in the face of adversity. Her doctor was optimistic, and seeing her like this, it was easy to share in that optimism.

As we chatted, the door opened and a nurse walked in. She was young, probably in her late twenties, with a bright and friendly demeanor. "Hello, everyone. I'm April Dawson, one of the nurses assigned to Amanda's case."

"Nice to meet you, April," Amanda said. "This is my brother, Zack, and his girlfriend, V."

April nodded at us, her smile unwavering. "It's wonderful to meet both of you," she said. Then, quickly dismissing us, she turned to her patient. "Amanda, I've heard from the other nurses that you are quite the fighter."

Amanda's cheeks flushed as she looked away shyly.

Nurse April checked Amanda's vitals, asking questions as she went. "So, Zack, you were the donor, right? That's such a brave thing to do. How are you feeling after the procedure?"

Zack shrugged modestly. "I'm okay. Just glad I could help."

The nurse's questions continued, delving into Zack's recovery process and his feelings about the transplant. Something about the way she probed, her intense focus on Zack, made me feel uneasy. Her questions seemed overly personal, not just the usual inquiries a nurse might make.

"Nurse, thank you for taking such good care of me," Amanda interjected, breaking the flow of questioning. "But I think my brother deserves a break from all the medical talk, don't you?"

The nurse laughed, a sound that seemed too cheery. "Of course, I'm sorry. And, please, call me April. Sometimes I get carried away, that's all. It's so heartwarming to see such a close bond between siblings."

She finished up her tasks and left the room, but the trace of discomfort lingered. It was probably nothing, just a nurse being thorough, yet my gut was doing somersaults.

As we continued our visit, I watched Amanda's interactions with Zack, the genuine affection and gratitude she had for him. It was a touching scene, but in the back of my mind, Nurse April tormented me, I just couldn't figure out why.

When it was time to leave, Amanda seemed disappointed. "You'll come back soon, right?"

"Of course," Zack promised, squeezing her hand. "We'll be here."

As we walked down the corridor, I glanced at Zack. He seemed lighter, more at ease after seeing Amanda doing well. I wanted to voice my unease about the nurse, but I held back, not wanting to be negative when the visit had been so positive, overall.

WE VISITED AMANDA SUNDAY, too. I offered to get everyone coffee and made sure I stayed gone a while to give Zack and Amanda a chance to catch up on each other's lives. When I came back, her husband, David, and their two girls were in the room. They looked like such a sweet family. I was glad Zack had been given this chance to reconnect with his sister, even if it meant he had to donate some bone marrow to make it happen. He was young and healthy, and recovering quickly. It seemed like a no brainer to me.

When it was time to leave, Zack told Amanda he had to work Monday but promised her he'd visit again after school on Tuesday. Only, he never got that chance.

On Tuesday morning, Zack's mom received an urgent call from the hospital. Something was wrong. Zack quickly called and filled me in, and I met them at the hospital. It was 7:36.

THE HOSPITAL WAITING room felt like a world suspended in time, dimly lit and shrouded in a silence that weighed heavily on my heart. I sat slightly apart from Zack's family, feeling like an intruder in their private universe of grief, yet compelled to be there by Zack's request. I watched them, a tight-knit circle of shared sorrow, each lost in their own thoughts, waiting for news about Amanda.

My gaze lingered on Zack. He sat, stoic and tense, the embodiment of a storm about to break. I remembered how his voice had trembled over the phone, asking me to come. Yet, I felt out of place, even though I knew my presence mattered to him.

The door swung open, and a doctor stepped in, his solemn expression mirroring the gravity of the moment. The room, already quiet, seemed to mute further. Everyone stood up, including me, feeling a knot tighten in my stomach. I watched the family's faces, seeing the flicker of hope in their eyes, daring to hope alongside them.

The doctor's words, delivered with a somber gentleness, shattered that fragile hope. "I have some difficult news to share," he began. "Despite initially responding well to the transplant, Amanda's condition took a sudden and severe turn for the worse. Her body, it seems, rejected the bone marrow cells. This led to multiple organ failure. We attempted every possible intervention, but unfortunately, we were unable to save her. Amanda didn't make it."

I felt the words like a physical blow, my heart aching for Zack and his family. I watched as the room absorbed the devastating news, the air growing heavier with the weight of their collective heartbreak. The straightforward delivery of the news was met with a stunned silence, as the finality of his words sank in.

Chloe's gasp cut through the silence, tears streaming down her face. Zack moved to her side, his own tears unrestrained. My eyes blurred with sympathy, feeling the raw pain that filled the room.

Zack's face was a mask of disbelief, tears carving tracks down his cheeks as he held his mother. David, Amanda's husband, stood frozen, a picture of utter devastation. My heart ached at the sight of the twins clinging to their father, too young to understand. Their innocent eyes were wide with confusion and fear.

Chloe's voice, laden with disbelief and pain, pierced the silence. "She didn't make it?" she asked, hoping she got something wrong.

"No, ma'am, Amanda died. I am so sorry for your loss," the

doctor continued, his voice compassionate but firm. "We're here for you, for anything you need."

Chloe sobbed, "Not my baby girl, not Amanda."

Zack's whispered denials, "No, no, no . . ." echoed in my ears, a haunting refrain.

I felt like an intruder witnessing such intimate sorrow, yet I couldn't leave. I was here for Zack, a silent pillar of support.

Chloe, supported by Zack, looked at the doctor, her face etched with pain. "Can we see her?" she asked, her voice breaking.

"Of course," the doctor replied gently. "Take all the time you need."

As the family moved toward Amanda's room, I hesitated, then followed at a distance, respecting their moment but staying close.

Inside, Amanda lay in serene contrast to the turmoil around her, looking still and peaceful. Chloe's touch on her daughter's hand, the flow of tears, spoke volumes. Zack, his gaze fixed on his sister, whispered a goodbye filled with love and unspoken words. Her family gathered around her, each person saying their silent farewells, their hearts heavy with the knowledge that this was the last time they would be together like this.

I stood by the doorway, my heart heavy, observing the family's grief. I realized then the profound impact of this moment, not just on them, but on me as well. This shared experience, though I was only a peripheral part of it, underscored life's fragility and the unyielding strength of family bonds. In that room, amid the sorrow, I understood the depth of Zack's pain and the immense role I played just by being there.

THE WEEK FOLLOWING Amanda's death was one of the longest and most somber I had ever experienced. The news had come as a huge shock, especially since she had been doing so well—and looked so healthy only days ago! No one had been prepared for this sudden tragedy.

As I sat down on Thursday night to take my third practice SAT test, my mind was elsewhere. The thought of Zack, his mom, and those little twin girls left without their mother, haunted me. Zack and Chloe had just gotten her back after all those years apart. And now she was gone again. Forever. Just like that. My heart hurt for them.

The test in front of me blurred into a mess of words and numbers, none of which could penetrate the fog of my grief. I tried to focus, but my thoughts kept drifting back to Zack and his family. How would they cope? How could they move on from such a profound loss?

As the week crawled by in a haze of sadness and routine, I spent most of my time trying to comfort Zack. He was alone because his mom was busy helping David with the funeral arrangements.

Amanda's funeral was set for Saturday, at 1 PM, in Ventura. It meant I had to skip my last Prepped class, but there was no question about where I needed to be. Ventura was at least a two-hour drive north, the place where Amanda had been close to her husband David's family.

The day of the funeral arrived, and the drive to Ventura was a quiet one. Chloe was lost in her thoughts as Zack drove, staring forward at the traffic ahead. I sat in the back, gazing out the window and feeling the profound sorrow of everyone in the car.

The funeral itself was heartbreakingly sad. The church was packed with Amanda's friends, many in their twenties, a reminder of how young she had been. David spoke a few words, his voice heavy with emotion.

"Thank you all for being here today to celebrate Amanda's life. Amanda was more than just my wife; she was my best friend, the mother of our beautiful girls, and a light in the lives of everyone she met."

I shot a furtive glance at Zack as he lowered his head, his eyes closed in a silent show of respect. Chloe reached over and held his hand, offering silent support.

David continued, "Amanda had an infectious laugh and a kind heart. She saw the good in people, always encouraging, always loving. She was passionate about her work, about helping others, and she brought joy to every room she entered."

There was a collective sigh from the congregation, a shared moment of grief and remembrance.

"To our twin girls, she was the world. She loved you more than anything, and she will always be with you, in the lessons she taught you, in the love she gave you."

David paused, taking a deep breath as he fought to keep his composure. "While we mourn her loss, we also celebrate the time we had with her. Amanda's legacy is one of love, laughter, and kindness. She may no longer be with us physically, but her spirit will live on in our hearts forever."

As he stepped down, there was a heavy silence, the kind that comes from words that hit close to home. Zack's face was a mask of stoic sorrow. I wanted to reach out, to offer some comfort, but I hesitated, unsure of my place in this moment of intimate family grief.

The service ended with a final prayer, and as we filed out of the church, the reality of Amanda's absence felt more poignant than ever.

After the service, there was a gathering for family at David's parents' house. Chloe initially hesitated, not wanting to impose, but David insisted we attend. The gathering was a mix of reminiscing and mourning, a bittersweet celebration of Amanda's life.

I felt out of place amid the intimate family setting. Zack, usually so full of life and warmth, was quiet, his usual spark dimmed by grief. I couldn't shake the feeling that he was withdrawing, pulling away not just from the world but from me too.

As the day wore on, I found myself questioning my presence there. Was I intruding on a deeply personal family moment? Did Zack even want me there? The doubts swirled in my mind, adding to the day's heavy emotions.

The ride back to Orange was silent, each of us lost in our thoughts. The day had been a harsh reminder of the impermanence of life and the unpredictable nature of our journey through it. As I lay in bed that night, the events of the day replayed in my mind, reminding me of the importance of cherishing every moment we have with our loved ones.

17

PINKTOBER AGAIN

The next morning, I woke to the persistent ringing of my phone and groggily squinted at the screen. An unfamiliar number flashed across it, so I ignored it. No sooner had I set the phone down than it buzzed with a text.

> Hey, V. It's Jenny, ASB (Associated Student Body) president. Sorry to bother you on a Sunday morning, but it's October 1st already and we're scrambling to plan the Pinktober month kickoff that starts tomorrow. We want to honor Mrs. J and we have a few things in mind. Do you want to help us out?

My first instinct was to reply with an emphatic 'NO!' I typed it but didn't hit send. I still vividly remembered how overwhelming everything had been two years ago with the whole 'Pinktober Girl' campaign for my mom. The community and school support she received had been incredible, but now, with her cancer returning, I couldn't bear the thought of going through that all over again. Plus, with Zack's sister having just died, my mind was a whirlwind of grief and frustration. Why did life have to be so relentlessly unfair?

I deleted my initial response and reconsidered.

> Zack's sister just died and I have a lot going on right now… but I'll help how I can. What do you want me to do?

I texted back, my heart heavy with mixed emotions. Jenny's reply came quickly:

> OMG! I'm so sorry! Never mind, you don't need to do a thing. We got this.

> Thanks 😊

I tossed my phone aside, a sense of dread building at the thought of facing school the next day, with its inevitable sea of pink and the suffocating weight of pitying glances. By the way, *I don't even like the color pink!* This was going to be a long PINKtober, with constant reminders of breast cancer awareness in my face all month.

I threw on a pair of sweats and dragged myself downstairs. To my shock and horror, Dad and Scotty were in the kitchen, making pancakes together. Completely out of the ordinary, alarm bells sounded in my head.

"What's going on? Where's Mom?" I asked, a note of panic creeping into my voice.

Dad, ever the optimist, greeted me cheerfully. "Good morning, sunshine. Would you like some pancakes?"

Scotty, his face smeared with chocolate, grinned up at me. "Dad let me put the chocolate chips in!"

I couldn't help but smile at his excitement, even as my

concern for Mom grew. "So?" I prompted Dad again, looking for answers.

"Mom is resting. She didn't sleep well last night," he replied, a little too casually.

I wasn't convinced. Something was wrong. I felt it in my gut. Without trying to get more out of Dad, I decided to find out for myself.

I headed straight to Mom's bedroom, where I found her tossing and turning in bed, a sheen of sweat on her forehead. She moaned in discomfort, her hands pressed against her abdomen.

"Mom, you're burning up!" I exclaimed, touching her forehead. "Dad! Get up here!"

The urgency of the situation kicked us into high gear. We managed to get Mom downstairs and into Dad's car. He rushed her to the ER while I stayed home with Scotty, trying to reassure him and myself that she'd be okay.

"Is she gonna be okay? I want Mommy!" Scotty cried. "I don't want her to be broken anymore."

"Oh, Scotty, no," I soothed, "she's not broken. The doctors are fixing her up right now. Besides, Mom's tough; you know that. She's just probably having a bad reaction to some of her medicine. She'll be fine."

AFTER ABOUT SIX HOURS, Mom returned from the ER, exhausted and still unwell. She spent the rest of the day in bed, too weak to go to work the next day.

Monday at school was a blur of whispers and sympathetic

looks. Emma caught up with me, concern etched on her face. "Hey V, how are you holding up?"

"I'm okay. Mom's strong. She'll get through this," I replied, not entirely convinced.

"Did Jenny get a hold of you yesterday about Pinktober?" she asked.

"Yeah, she did. Why, did she rope you into helping her?"

Emma nodded. "How could I say no? It's for my best friend's mom. Besides, I want to help." She smiled reassuringly.

"Thank you, Emma. You really are the best friend anyone could ever have."

Ignoring my sappiness, Emma excitedly told me about the planning meeting she'd had with Jenny and the student council. "We're going to have a 'Walk for Pinktober,' a charity walk around the school track. Everyone will wear pink ribbons and matching T-shirts. We got the art club and music department to pitch in with making banners and posters, and the band even promised a live performance."

I was taken aback by how quickly they had organized everything. "Wow, that was fast! I don't know what to say. Mom is going to love it."

"Do you think she'll be back by this Friday?" Emma asked, hopeful.

I sighed. "I don't know. It's hard to say. I'm not sure what's wrong this time."

Walking through the halls, adorned with pink ribbons and posters, I felt a mix of gratitude and sorrow. The Pinktober event was a beautiful gesture, but it also served as a reminder of the uncertain journey we were on with my mom's health.

THANKFULLY, Mom felt well enough to go back to work Tuesday. The hallways were a cascade of pink—ribbons, posters, and decorations the Walkathon committee had put up for Pinktober. Mom, unlike me, basked in the sea of pink. She moved through the halls with a renewed vigor, her smile brighter than I'd seen in days. It was as if the pink tide and the students' support were infusing her with energy and strength.

This uplifting atmosphere lightened my spirits, especially since tonight was crucial; it was my last practice SAT test before the real deal on Saturday. Missing the final Prepped class for Amanda's funeral had set me back, but Emma had been a lifesaver. She handed me her detailed notes, and we spent every spare moment—lunch and the hours after school—holed up in the library, pouring over test strategies and problem-solving techniques.

As the time for the practice test neared, I felt a jittery mix of readiness and apprehension. This was it, my final rehearsal. But there was another layer to this evening—it was also my last opportunity to keep an eye on Jacob's flock. The mystery of their SAT cheating scheme was like an itch I couldn't scratch, and tonight I hoped to catch a glimpse of their plan.

Arriving for the practice test, I was surprised to find Lucas Bennett absent. In his place was a substitute, a change that struck me as odd. He had always been so invested in our progress, so his absence on this final gathering seemed out of character. Didn't he want to see us off, give us some final words of encouragement? The missing piece of this puzzle added another layer of intrigue to the evening.

Despite the distraction of our instructor's absence and my suspicions about the cheating ring, I managed to focus on the test. I worked through each section with a steady determination, drawing on all the knowledge and tactics Emma and I had reviewed.

When I finished, I felt a cautious sense of satisfaction. My score wasn't perfect, but it was solid. A 1390 was within reach, which would put me comfortably above the 90th percentile, a respectable place to be. As I packed up my things, I heard Jacob's crew. They were speaking in hushed tones, excitement in their voices. But without any concrete evidence, I was left to speculate and wait.

Walking out of the classroom, I felt a mix of emotions . . . relief the practice tests were over, anxiety about the taking the actual SAT, and frustration that I knew others were cheating, and I felt powerless to stop it. How could I prove Jacob cheated? No one would believe me unless I could get evidence. I was obsessing over this. But it took my mind off other worries, like Zack's withdrawing and my mom's health. At least, whatever happened on Saturday, I would do my best. And for now, that would have to be good enough.

18

A WALK FOR HOPE

Friday dawned with a flurry of emotions and activities as Sierra High geared up for the big fundraising walk for breast cancer. School was on a minimum day schedule in honor of the event, which was especially meaningful since it was dedicated to my mom and her fight against breast cancer.

I stepped onto the school track at 1:15 p.m., amazed at the sea of people who had shown up. The track was a splendid array of pink. Students, teachers, and community members were all donned in various shades of the color, from soft pastels to vibrant fuchsias. The Orange Fire Department brought out their pink firetruck again, a crowd favorite, surrounded by banners and balloons fluttering in the breeze.

But the festive energy of the day was marred by the news I received at 11:30 that morning. Mom had been rushed to the ER again with the same abdominal pains as before. My heart sank, knowing she wouldn't be there to see the event that had been put together in her honor. I tried to keep a brave face, but how could I not be disappointed?

The walk, however, was amazing. We began with a moment of silence, then the sound of a starting horn set us off. I walked alongside Emma, my own private cheerleader who kept my spirits up with every lap around that track. We were surrounded by a community united for a cause. It was inspiring to see so many people come together, but my mind was on my mom.

Throughout the event, I sent Mom and Dad texts and pictures, trying to bring a piece of the walk to her in the hospital. She called me.

"Hi, sweetie. I won't keep you. I just wanted to tell you I'm so proud of you and I wish I could be there."

"I know, Mom. You're here in spirit. We're all walking for you. Anything you want to say to the crowd?"

"Oh absolutely, you know me," she replied with a hint of mischief. "I'll text it to you so you don't have to memorize it." The phone clicked and I realized she'd hung up on me. A few seconds later, the text came in she wanted me to share with everyone.

MOM

I love you all! Thank you so very much—your support means EVERYTHING to me. I'm fighting strong, Warriors! Mountains and mountains of love! ~Mrs. J

As I read her words aloud to the crowd, everyone applauded, some with tears in their eyes. I was overwhelmed by the love and support for my brave and resilient mother.

Jenny took the microphone. "Today we walk for Mrs. J, our Pinktober Girl. She's taught us more than just literature; she's taught us about strength, courage, and hope."

More applause. I felt a tear slide down my cheek. Emma squeezed my hand, her support unspoken but deeply felt.

Later that afternoon, the crushing news came. Mom needed emergency surgery the next morning... the same morning as my SAT. My world spun. How was I supposed to focus on a test when my mom would be in surgery? The frustration and help-lessness I felt were almost more than I could bear.

After the walkathon wrapped up, I visited her in the hospi-tal. She was weak but determined, insisting that I take the SAT.

"There's no reason for you to waste your time in a hospital waiting room, sweetie. I'm going to be fine," she said. Her insis-tence only added to my inner turmoil. *What should I do?*

That night, I turned to Zack for comfort, but he was with-drawn, lost in his own grief since Amanda's death. It seemed as if he were retreating, burdened by a misplaced guilt. I wanted to help him, to ease his pain, but I didn't know how.

I spent the night tossing and turning, sleep eluding me. The SAT, the cheating scandal—they seemed so trivial now. All I wanted was for my mom to be okay and for Zack to find his smile again. Why did everything have to be so complicated? Why couldn't life just be normal for once?

THE FIRST LIGHT of Saturday morning didn't bring clarity, just a bucketload of worries and a decision I wasn't ready to make. The day ahead was like a dark cloud on the horizon, full of challenges I couldn't predict or control.

Dragging myself out of bed, I trudged over to my wall. There it was, the date circled in an accusing red Sharpie:

"SATs TODAY!"

As if I could forget. But as I stared at the daunting words, a realization settled in. The SATs would go on, in classrooms across the country, but without me.

My phone buzzed in my pocket as I sat in the too-quiet hospital waiting room with Dad. We didn't need to talk; he understood the score without me saying a word.

Earlier, I'd roused Scotty out of bed with the promise of a whole day with his best friend, Alex. After dropping him off, I picked up two coffees from our favorite barista and headed to the hospital. Dad was grateful for the gesture, after spending a sleepless night in Mom's hospital room, unable to leave her side.

I pulled out my phone to see Emma's text lighting up the screen.

> Where are you? The test is about to start!

I stared at the message, torn. How could I explain that being here, in this cold, impersonal hospital, waiting for news on my mom's surgery, was where I needed to be? More important than any test.

Mom's emergency surgery was no small deal. It was a major operation to remove the part of her colon that kept getting infected. Even though she'd pushed me to go take the SAT, there was no way. Not while she was in the OR. I made the right choice, and I'd make it again.

I was lost in a sea of blank hospital walls when my phone buzzed again. This time, it was a message from Mom to her co-teacher, Miss Tisdale, forwarded to me:

MISS TISDALE (FORWARDED FROM HANNAH)

I'm all right but frustrated. Been through 6 antibiotics and to the ER a couple times. And now this surgery. UGH.

At first, I didn't get why Miss Tisdale sent this. Then it clicked. After our heart-to-heart about mortality and my search for the truth, she was probably trying to give me a window into my mom's world.

Reading the text again, I was hit with a wave of helplessness, but also a deep respect for my mom's grit. She'd always been a fighter, facing each challenge head-on. And here I was, unable to tear myself away from her side, not even for a few hours.

The waiting room felt like a time warp, every minute dragging on forever. Nurses moved in and out, their faces a study in calm professionalism. I tried to lose myself in a book, but the words just danced meaninglessly before my eyes.

Finally, after what seemed an eternity, a surgeon in blue scrubs approached. "Carlos?"

Dad and I stood together, afraid to breathe.

"She's out of surgery, and everything went well. She'll be in recovery for a while, but you should be able to see her soon."

A wave of relief washed over us. "Thank you," Dad whispered, his voice hoarse with emotion.

As I sat back down, my mind replayed Mom's text. Her frustration, her repeated trips to the ER, her fighting spirit . . . it all culminated in this moment of relief. I knew the road ahead would be long and challenging, but right then, all that mattered was that she was safe.

I finally texted Emma back.

I'm with Mom at the hospital. She's out of surgery, and it went well. 🩶

The SAT, an ominous milestone just yesterday, seemed trivial now. I was exactly in the right place—by my mom's side, ready to support her through her recovery, just as she had always been there for me.

19

UNVEILED WORDS

While Mom was still in the hospital, Dad asked for my help in cleaning the house. He wanted everything to be perfect for her return on Tuesday. Dutifully, I started in their bedroom, gathering a pile of dirty towels and laundry. As I reached into the closet to pick up their laundry basket, my eyes fell upon a hardcover book leaning against the wall. *That's odd. What's this doing here?* Curiosity piqued, I picked up the book and opened it.

It was a journal, bound in a simple yet elegant cloth cover with pages and pages of my mom's handwriting. This was her private world, her thoughts and feelings captured in ink. The sight of her writing felt both intimate and invasive. I snapped the journal shut, not wanting to invade her privacy. I put the journal back on the closet floor and left with the laundry.

But nagging thoughts haunted me all afternoon. Was she still hiding things from me? What secrets were penned in those pages? The need to understand her, to gauge the severity of her disease, overpowered me.

Later that evening, telling Dad I had homework, I retreated

to my room with the journal tucked safely under my arm. I carefully placed it behind my pillow, rationalizing that I would only read a couple of pages before returning it to its secret spot.

Twenty minutes later, I sat on my bed and gently opened the journal. The first entry greeted me, my mom's handwriting a familiar comfort.

I began to read, each word pulling me deeper into her experiences, her struggles, her fears, and her hopes. Page by page, I journeyed through her thoughts, feeling closer to her than ever before. The words painted a picture of her inner strength, her determination, and, at times, her vulnerability.

I felt a mixture of emotions . . . love, admiration, sadness, and a newfound understanding. It was as if, through her words, I was seeing my mom in a whole new light. Her courage, her fierce love for my dad, brother, and me, her determination to fight—it was all there, raw and unfiltered.

When I closed the journal, I felt a new closeness to her. I had discovered a part of my mom I had never known, a depth that only made me admire her more. It also reignited my determination to be there for her, to support her in her battle, just as she had always been there for me.

I placed the journal back in its hidden spot. I didn't need it. Her words would stay with me . . . they were forever etched in my heart.

Whispers from Hanna's Diary

I crazily decided to go back to work! And the days I have been able to teach in August and September have been WONDERFUL. I fell in love with the students on day one--they are amazing kids. I had some time off from treatment at the end of summer and then started a new chemo, adriamycin (the "red devil"), in August. Unfortunately my cancer markers are climbing and they have more than tripled since July. This means that the current chemo is not working. Also, my liver function is abnormal so Dr. Khatri has ordered an MRI for next week, and based on the results we will decide which therapy to pursue at that point. She is looking at a combination of two different chemo's. This is a big set-back, and of course I'm terrified. But I hope and hope and hope and pray that the next one we try will knock it out once again. I won't give up. I won't ever give up.

...I just got off the phone with my insurance company for prescriptions and they won't cover a single cent of the new drug I'm being prescribed. I can't understand how Stage IV cancer doesn't qualify me for any drug that could possibly extend my life. Especially this one at $5,000 a month. I've had an MRI of my brain, CAT scans of my chest and abdomen, and a bone scan tomorrow. My insurance denied a PET scan—the test that would be the most helpful! UGH!

...My insurance still denies Ibrance, the drug that keeps me alive. The amount of time I have spent on the phone with them makes me want to pull my hair out!! That is, what little hair I have left. And I'm fighting this fight while also trying to be a mom, a teacher, and a wife.

...*Update! This time I'm celebrating GOOD news! I had my oncology appointment yesterday to go over the MRI, scans, and follow up X-ray. All the tests indicated NO new metastasis!!!! Hooray! As for the spike in my cancer markers, a PET scan would best determine where there is any cancer, but it's still denied by insurance, so we're re-submitting the request and will continue to appeal. The bone pain I'm experiencing is a rough side effect from the letrozole (anti-hormone medicine), so that explains the chest/sternum and back pain. It's something I just have to live with—but I can do that! This is all great news!*

...*Tough news. I finally got my PET scan yesterday and met with Dr. Khatri to discuss the results. Even though my recent tests all came back good, the PET scan is what really shows where the cancer is. Several lymph nodes lit up—meaning cancer—in my chest and on my neck. The good news is that my lungs, brain, organs, and bones showed NOTHING (hooray!). The cancer has "woken up" in the areas where it initially was when I was first diagnosed. This is most likely because I've been forced to take a break from the Ibrance. I'm in crying mode today but come tomorrow I'll be the same stubborn red-headed fighting crazy mom wife teacher and friend. Always! Fuck Cancer.*

...*I have GOOD NEWS!! Insurance will finally cover my Ibrance! Dr. Khatri's nurse called and told me I should be hearing from them soon—HOORAY!!!! I believe it was* a community effort with so many people offering help, suggestions and prayers, not to mention my stubborn refusal to accept the denials. Now I can go back on it and let it do its job!

...The cancer has progressed to my bones, neck, and liver. I'm sad and devastated, terrified and confused. But I still have hope. I won't give up, ever. I'm as stubborn and feisty as the day Carlos married me, and I'm not going anywhere. I will find a way to beat this again with all the strength and love that everyone has shared with me and my family. I hold it in my heart every single moment of every single day. And it will carry me through this fight. I will most likely start chemo again, the same regimen and meds I did when I was first diagnosed. I'm PISSED I have to lose my hair again—it was looking so red and unruly and I kind of fell in love with it. I imagine that it will come back with a vengeance though, hopefully even curlier and crazier than this last time. My treatments will affect the family a bit harder this time . . .

...Dr. confirmed that chemo second time around is much harder, so it will be a "see as we go" mentality. In other words, how long I can tolerate it as long as it's working. After the second or third round she will order a scan to see if it's doing the job. I'll continue with a shot every four weeks that strengthens my bones. That is super important. Basic pathology from the liver biopsy shows that it's nearly the same beast, estrogen receptor positive, but it has most likely mutated to "outsmart" my hormone therapy. I'm looking at some form of chemo for at least a year, and then we will see what else comes along or gets approved. Sigh. I am fighting mad and I have to remember that this is a MARATHON. I am in it for the long haul! I refuse to be beaten down by this. I am not defined by my disease. I cannot be gotten rid of that easily! I am strong. I am fierce. I can do this.

20
A TEACHER'S DEDICATION

When Mom was released from the hospital two days later, her doctors sent her home with firm instructions that she rest at home for at least five weeks. When I got home from school, I overheard her and Dad talking in the kitchen.

"I just don't know how I'll manage being away from school for so long," Mom said. "You know I've already used up all my sick days."

"Babe, you need to focus on getting better," Dad said. "That's the most important thing right now."

I heard her sigh. "I know, honey. It's just hard. At least I've been cleared for short-term disability leave, so that's something, I guess."

"Hannah, I know you're frustrated. But rest assured, your students are in good hands. Jessica is a Godsend and the kids love her."

"I know. I'm so blessed but—"

"No buts." Dad chuckled. "Come on, let's get you upstairs and in bed. Doctor's orders."

It was true, Mom had been lucky to get Jessica Tisdale as a co-teacher and long-term substitute. Miss Tisdale was young, enthusiastic, and had quickly become a favorite among the students. Even Zack said she was great.

On instinct, I quickly ducked in the laundry room so my parents wouldn't know I'd been eavesdropping. It was silly, I knew, but I just thought they deserved a little privacy in that moment. I waited until they were both upstairs before coming back out.

Over the next few days and weeks I caught Mom texting or calling poor Miss Tisdale, over and over. True to her own description of herself, my mom was a stubborn redhead in every sense of the word.

"Mom, are you micro-managing your classes from your sickbed?" I teased one afternoon.

"Guilty as charged. But Jessica is doing wonderfully. I just can't help but want to be involved."

Mom's dedication to her job went beyond the confines of the classroom. It was clear she genuinely cared about her students, her colleagues, and her role as an educator.

So when the next Pinktober fundraiser in her honor was announced, her reaction was one of surprise and delight.

During the announcements Friday morning, my mom's best friend and fellow English teacher, Rebecca Nichols, got on the intercom:

"On Monday, I will be joining several other Sierra teachers to raise money for Hannah Jiménez by accepting the Pink Hair

Challenge issued by our ASB. If enough money is raised to support the wonderful Jiménez family, I will dye my hair pink. Please give generously if you want to see me and other teachers go pink for an amazing cause! Donation buckets will be in the quad all next week with our names on them."

Then the ASB president, Jenny Ngo, got on the intercom:

"Thank you, Mrs. Nichols. Keep an eye on our school website's page for updates as new teachers join the contest. Please donate generously toward the teacher you would most like to see with pink hair for Mrs. J! The challenge begins Monday."

When I got home and shared the news with Mom about the school's Pink Hair Challenge, she loved the idea.

"Can you imagine Mr. Sutton with pink hair?" She giggled, the sparkle returning to her eyes.

"Now that I have to see! I'll definitely be taking pictures!" I replied.

Not one to keep quiet, Mom quickly grabbed her phone, jumped on the school's website and commented:

"Oh my gosh! Sierra is turning PINK! I love love love you my Sierra staff friends! You have no idea how much this makes my day, makes me stronger, and makes me want to kick a**!!! Thank you from every part of my heart and soul.

Mountains of love, Hannah #fightstrong #hannahsheroes"

I gave Mom a gentle hug and excused myself to get ready. Emma and I had a big 'date' to attend the Homecoming football game together. Zack couldn't go with us because he had to work, but he promised to take me to the Homecoming dance Saturday night.

21

HOMECOMING

Saturday night had finally rolled around, and it was time for the Homecoming dance—the high school social event of the season. The buzz from our football team trouncing Orange High the night before still hung in the air like electric static at Sierra High. The school was practically vibrating with adrenaline and excitement.

Zack and I strolled into the transformed gym, hand in hand, which had been given the full Cinderella treatment. Twinkling lights, shimmering decorations, and balloons in our school colors of red, white, and black, intertwined with streamers, seemed to dance all around us. The "Go Warriors!" banner was like a victory flag, waving proudly over the entrance.

I was dressed in a champagne-colored spaghetti strap minidress, a choice that felt both glamorous and slightly out of my element. The wedge heels I'd picked, the only ones that didn't clash horribly with my dress, were a reminder of my general dislike for all non-sneaker footwear.

Dancing with Zack, I felt a wave of comfort wash over me. His presence was familiar and grounding, a much-needed anchor. He'd been kind of distant since Amanda's death, and with everything going on with my mom, so we hadn't had much us-time lately.

"You look beautiful tonight, V," he murmured, his voice almost lost in the music.

I looked up at him, feeling a surge of warmth. "Thanks, Zack. Tonight feels just right."

His smile was a knockout, and for a split second, it felt like we were alone in our own world.

But then, like a record scratch in a movie scene, I felt an unwelcome jolt. Jacob "accidentally" collided with me, his glare sharp enough to cut glass even in the dim gym lighting. My blood boiled, but I reined it in. This wasn't the place for a showdown.

Zack, caught up in the moment, missed it entirely. "What's wrong?" he asked, picking up on my sudden tension.

"Just a little chilly," I lied, tugging at my dress, not wanting to drag him into my ongoing Jacob drama.

As the evening unfolded, I tried to lock away thoughts of Jacob and his antics. Emma, always my confidant, listened to my concerns with a furrowed brow. We agreed to keep it between us, not wanting to involve Zack in what might be turning into a dangerous cat-and-mouse game.

The night had its high points—laughter, dancing, friends, and the usual shenanigans. But Jacob's dark cloud lingered in the back of my mind.

As the night wound down and Zack took me home, I was relieved to leave the dance's emotional rollercoaster. But that relief evaporated when I saw it. Stepping onto my front porch, in the soft glow of the porch light, lay a dead rat. Its lifeless form grotesquely out of place against the tidy backdrop of my front yard. A shiver skittered down my spine.

Was this another message from Jacob? Or just a freak occurrence?

I rushed inside, not wanting to think about it any longer. That night, I hit the pillow with a heart weighed down by determination and concern. How far was I willing to go for the truth, and at what cost to those around me?

MONDAY, the quad was buzzing with excitement as I walked through, the air filled with a sense of purpose and camaraderie. My school had always been a tight-knit community, but today, it felt like more than that. Today, we were a family, united for a cause close to all our hearts.

At the center of the quad were tables adorned with pink streamers and donation buckets, each labeled with the name of a teacher participating in the Pink Hair Challenge. The challenge was simple yet powerful: raise enough money and these teachers would dye their hair pink in honor of Mrs. J, my mom Hannah Jiménez, who was bravely battling cancer.

Emma spotted me from across the crowd and waved me over. "V, look at this! Nearly all the teachers are participating. Even Mr. Sutton, can you believe it?"

I smiled at seeing Mr. Sutton's name on one of the buckets. Known for his strict demeanor and no-nonsense approach to teaching, seeing him volunteer to dye his hair pink was the last thing I'd expect him to do.

"It's amazing," I replied, my eyes scanning the quad. Students from all grades were there, dropping their donations into the buckets. Many were even wearing pink ribbons or T-shirts in support.

"Your mom has touched so many lives here, V," Emma said softly. "Look at what she's inspired."

I felt a lump form in my throat as I looked around. Teachers, students, even some parents who had come to show their support, were all here for my mom. She wasn't just a teacher at Sierra High; she was part of the school's heart and soul.

Just then, Principal Fitzgibbon appeared on the makeshift stage set up near the tables. "Good morning, Warriors!" he boomed into the microphone, and the crowd quieted down. "This week, we come together for one of our own. Mrs. Jiménez, or Mrs. J as many of you know her, has been a beacon of strength and inspiration in our community."

He continued, talking about the challenge and the cause, but my mind drifted to Mom. She was at home, probably grading papers or writing lesson plans for Miss Tisdale, unaware of the movement she had sparked here.

"We are more than just a school; we are a community that looks after its own. Let's show Mrs. J just how much we stand with her!" Principal Fitzgibbon concluded, his words met with cheers and applause.

As the crowd dispersed, I peeked into each donation bucket. The amount of money already collected was astounding. This was more than a fundraiser; it was a testament to the impact one person could have on so many lives. This was Sierra High at its best—showing strength, unity, and love. As I walked away, a smile spread across my face, imagining the sea of pink hair that would flood the school next week.

This was for you, Mom. We were all with you, every step of the way.

22

SURPRISE SUPER SCORES

Later that week, the halls at school were bustling with the usual between-class chatter and chaos. I was lost in thought about Zack and my mom, my mind a million miles away, staring blankly at the contents of my locker. When I slammed it shut, there he was—Jacob, leaning against the locker next to mine like some sort of brooding, unwelcome guardian angel.

"Did you like my present?" he sneered, the malice in his voice unmistakable.

I played it cool, meeting his gaze with a blank stare.

The rest of the world seemed to mute as he leaned in, his words a low hiss that sent a chill through me. "I'd be careful if I were you. We've got a rat problem at this school. It'd be a shame if I had to kill another one. Stop playing detective. This doesn't concern you."

I tried to keep my face a mask of calm, but inside, I was a tangle of nerves. "I don't know what you're talking about, Jacob," I said, my voice a tightrope walk of feigned ignorance and rising panic.

His eyes narrowed into slits. "Don't play dumb, V. You're poking around about the SATs. You think I don't know?"

The eyes of nearby students were on us, curious about our charged standoff. Jacob was blocking my escape, standing there like some kind of human roadblock.

"I'm just interested in . . . fair play," I countered, trying to inject a dose of confidence into my voice, despite the fear nipping at my heels.

Jacob's laugh was short and humorless. "Fair play? Is that what you call it? Listen, V, you're in way over your head. This is your only warning. Back off, or you'll regret it."

His words hung in the air between us. The threat unmistakable. For a brief moment, I felt a real sense of danger. Then, as quickly as he had appeared, Jacob walked away, his point made. He scanned the hallway, a predator making sure his territory was still secure as he swaggered off.

I stood there, taking a moment to collect myself. Jacob's threat was crystal clear, but it only fueled my determination. If he was this desperate to scare me off, he was definitely hiding something. I knew I had to tread carefully, but I also knew I couldn't just let this go. This was more than just a simple case of cheating on a test. There was a story here, and I was going to uncover it.

SATURDAY AFTERNOON, I was sprawled on my bed, deep in a novel, when my phone buzzed to life. It was a text from Emma that had my adrenaline kicking into high gear.

> V, mind-blowing news! Scored 1485 on my SATs!!!!!

> WOOHOO!!!! Epic! Congrats!

I texted back, a grin spreading across my face.

> Yep. 730 verbal 755 math

> Dang, you aced Math!

> Yeah! But something's fishy. Some of Jacob's crew got crazy high scores. And one girl from Prepped got 1590! We need to talk.

This was it, the break I'd been waiting for. I fired back,

> GET OVER HERE. Let's crack this.

Moments later, Emma burst into my room, her eyes wide with excitement and fear. She shoved her phone at me. The group chat from our Prepped class was a whirlwind of scores that screamed foul play.

"It doesn't add up, Emma," I said, my detective brain kicking into overdrive. "Jacob's perfect score was just the tip of the iceberg. We've stumbled onto something big."

Emma paced, her voice tinged with anxiety. "But these scores, V! I can't compete with these. What if they're legit? Should I retake the test and try to get a higher score?"

"Emma, stop. Your score is stellar, and more importantly, it's honest. Don't you see? These other scores are too neat, too perfect. It's a cover-up," I argued, feeling the pieces starting to align. "There's a pattern here we're missing."

Emma hesitated, then nodded. "I'll check their social media, see if there's any dirt on their study habits."

"Good idea. And I'm going to tail Jacob. He's the key," I declared, feeling the thrill of the hunt.

"But be careful, V. If they're cheating and they know we're onto them . . ." Emma's voice trailed off, her concern all over her face.

I gave her a resolute nod. "It's about more than just scores now. It's about integrity and fairness. We won't let them trample over the hard work of honest students like you."

"Thanks, V. But what about you? When are you taking the SATs?" Emma's tone was half worried, half incredulous.

"What do you mean?" I played dumb.

"You know exactly what I mean." Emma's gaze was piercing. "Since you bailed on our test day, have you rescheduled?"

"Oh, right. Yeah, of course. I'm aiming for spring, first Saturday in March. Just need things to cool off a bit."

Emma shot me a skeptical look.

"I mean it, promise."

"Okay. Let me know if you want to hit the books again before then. I'll keep my notes. March seems like a lifetime away right now."

"Thanks, Em. I'll definitely take you up on that." I grinned, feeling a mix of gratitude and resolve.

After Emma left, I felt a wave of determination wash over me. This wasn't just a hunt for the truth anymore; it was a fight for justice. And I was all in.

TEACHERS IN TECHNICOLOR

Walking into school Monday morning felt like plunging into a vivid pink ocean. Everywhere I looked, there was an explosion of color, more vibrant and livelier than anything I'd ever seen before. The halls were transformed into a gallery of solidarity, adorned with posters featuring our teachers. Each poster was a unique tribute—quotes, photos, artistic renditions—all unified by one striking feature: pink hair! At the bottom of each poster, the hashtag #HannahsHeroes gleamed, a beacon of collective support for my mom.

Navigating through the corridors, I was enveloped by a wave of enthusiasm from a team of pink-haired teachers. Their smiles were wide, their fists pumped in the air with a spirit of defiance against adversity. Warm wishes for Mom flowed from every corner. This wasn't an ordinary Monday; it was a heartfelt tribute, a day where the school's heartbeat synchronized with my mom's . . . with mine.

Teachers and students alike flaunted shades of pink in their hair, a spectrum ranging from soft pastels to bold magentas.

Even Mr. Sutton, the usually stern-faced Pre-Calc teacher, had his white hair dyed in a striking shade of fuchsia, his usual sternness replaced by a spirited grin. The air was electric with excitement, palpable and contagious, as everyone snapped photos and shared them on social media, creating a digital tapestry of support.

But amid this sea of celebration, a tide of overwhelming emotions pulled at me. Seeking refuge, I found myself drifting away from Zack and Emma under the guise of an off-campus errand. My steps led me to a familiar haven—Miss Torres's classroom. She had been more than just my English teacher last year; she was the one who guided me through the turbulence of my anger. Her words had been a lighthouse in my stormiest days, and her promise that her door was always open echoed in my mind.

Feeling apprehensive, I knocked lightly, my heart aflutter with a quiet desperation. "Miss Torres?" I called out, ready to unravel the knots of emotions that had tightened within me.

"Yes, come in," she replied, her voice warm and inviting. Miss Torres looked up from her desk, her hair a vivid shade of dark pink that seemed out of character for her usually reserved demeanor. "Well hello, V. It's so good to see you. What do you think of my pink hair? I rather like it, don't you?"

"No, I don't!" I blurted out, my voice breaking. "It's all just too much. Everyone's so cheerful, but I'm just . . . falling apart. My mom's sick AGAIN. Does it get better? Easier? How do you deal with it? My mom . . . is she . . . ?" The questions tumbled out, each one heavier than the last.

Miss Torres sighed softly, her expression turning solemn. She motioned for me to take a seat. "V, I won't lie to you. It's tough. When my dad died, I felt lost, like I was drifting in a sea of uncertainty and pain. But here's something I learned: it's okay to not be okay."

She paused, choosing her words with care. "Your mom's illness, it's a storm you're navigating. And it's alright to feel overwhelmed, to feel angry or sad. These emotions don't make you weak; they make you human."

"But how do you keep going?" I asked, my voice barely above a whisper.

"By embracing the little moments, all the joy and love you can," she said gently. "In times like these, we realize how precious each day is. The pink hair, the laughter, the support— it's all a way of creating light in the darkness. And it's okay to let yourself be a part of that, to let it lift you, even if it's just for a moment."

Her eyes met mine, filled with an understanding that only comes from experiencing loss. "And V, be honest with your feelings. Share them with people who care about you. You're not alone in this."

Her words sank in, a much needed solace to the chaos in my mind. "Thank you, Miss Torres. I . . . I needed to hear that."

As I stood to leave, she added, "Remember, V, it's okay to lean on others. And it's okay to celebrate life, even when it's hard. Your mom wants that for you."

Walking out of Miss Torres's classroom, I felt a weight lifted off my shoulders. It wasn't a magic solution to all my problems, but it was a start. Maybe I could find a way to be part of the pink, even just for today.

After leaving Miss Torres's classroom, I felt a bit steadier, like I could breathe again. The lunch period was nearly over, but I needed to see Zack and Emma before heading back to class. I spotted them at our usual table, engrossed in a quiet conversation.

When I approached, Emma looked up and knew something was off. "V, you okay?"

I managed a small smile. "Yeah, I just needed a moment, you know? But I'm ready to join the pink now." The words felt like a commitment, a step toward something positive amid my internal chaos.

Without a word, Emma excitedly rummaged through her backpack and produced a pink breast cancer ribbon and two pink hair extensions. "Here, let me help you put these on."

I bowed my head, allowing her to weave the extensions into my hair. The gentle touch was comforting, grounding. As she finished, I looked at the ribbon in my hand, its color now a symbol of more than just awareness—it was a symbol of unity, of standing together. Overwhelmed by gratitude, I wrapped Emma in a big hug.

"Thanks, Em. This means a lot," I murmured.

I then turned to Zack, noticing he was wearing a pink T-shirt. His support was there, but his eyes were distant, clouded with his own grief. The loss of his sister still hung heavily around him, an unspoken shadow that lingered in his quiet, reserved demeanor.

"Hey, Zack," I said gently. "I like your shirt. Thanks for being a part of this."

He offered a small, somewhat forced smile, a faint glimmer of his usual vibrant personality. "Yeah, of course," he replied softly. "I love your mom." His words were few, but in them, I heard the effort it took to be present, to be part of our world when his own was shattered.

At the end of lunch, we gathered our things and headed in different directions. As I walked to class, I felt the weight of the hair extensions on my head, a physical reminder of the support surrounding me. I pinned the ribbon to my shirt. It wasn't just a piece of fabric; it was a thread connecting me to everyone who cared, to a community that stood strong in the face of adversity. And though Zack's silence spoke of his own battle, his presence was proof of the strength we all carried, the strength to keep going, even when everything inside us was breaking.

24

PAWS AND REFLECT

By the time I got home from school and filled Mom in on the day's festivities, Dad arrived with Scotty. Even though we were at the same school, I rarely saw my dad there. So, when he walked into their bedroom donning a pink clown wig, Mom and I had to hold our stomachs as tears of laughter streamed down our faces. Dad's playful spirit was out in full force, and he loved to make Mom laugh.

I could sense he wanted some time with Mom, so I quickly suggested, "Scotty, why don't we take Lucky to the dog park?"

"A dog park? Oh boy, Lucky would love that!" Scotty's eyes lit up with excitement, his previous worries momentarily forgotten.

"Mom, can we go to Dog Beach?" I asked, hoping she'd agree.

"Please, Mommy! Pleeeeease?" Scotty joined in, his plea irresistible.

Mom nodded with a smile, though her eyes held a touch of fatigue. "It's okay with me, but make sure your dad writes you a note for driving Scotty."

"Yay! You hear that, Lucky? V's gonna take us to Dog Beach!" Scotty's cheer was contagious.

I organized our little outing, telling Scotty to get Lucky's leash and dog treats while I grabbed some waters and the Frisbee. The drive to the beach was a smooth twenty minutes, filled with Scotty's excited chatter and Lucky's eager whines.

Once we arrived and set Lucky free, his joy was unmistakable. He dashed toward the other dogs, wagging his tail furiously. Scotty and I laughed, watching the dogs play in the gentle surf, the shallow waves lapping over their paws.

Energized by the scene, Scotty and I kicked off our flip-flops and raced toward the water. The sand was warm under our feet, and we couldn't resist splashing each other as we ran. Scotty, with his endless energy and innocent laughter, reminded me of simpler times. We played tag, built sand castles, and threw the Frisbee for Lucky, who leapt with grace and enthusiasm.

As the sun began to dip toward the horizon, painting the sky in hues of orange and purple, I knew it was time to head back. "Come on, Scotty, let's get Lucky and head home."

The drive back was quiet, a comfortable silence filled with a sense of contentment. I glanced at Scotty in the backseat, who had fallen asleep, his head resting against the window, Lucky snoring softly at his side.

Pulling into the driveway, I felt a peace wash over me. Miss Torres was right—there's joy in the little moments. Today was a reminder that life isn't just about the challenges we face; it's also about these pockets of happiness, these brief escapes that remind us of the beauty in the world.

As I helped Scotty get in the house, his sleepy smile told me everything I needed to know, that today had been a good day, a day of simple joys and cherished memories. And for now, that was enough.

AFTER THE UPLIFTING day at Dog Beach with Scotty and Lucky, I found myself carrying a renewed sense of energy into the rest of the week. It was as if the laughter and the sea breeze had blown away some of the heavier clouds hanging over me.

Tuesday was the start of our Halloween preparations. The house, usually subdued, began to transform under our hands into a spooky wonderland. Scotty bubbled with excitement amid the Halloween buzz.

"Look, V! Can we put the giant spider on the front porch this year?" Scotty asked, holding up an impressively large, fake spider that seemed to have more eyes than necessary.

"Absolutely, that'll scare off any unwanted ghosts," I replied with a grin, hoisting the spider into place. Its long, furry legs dangled ominously over the porch railing.

As the week progressed, our home continued to evolve. We strung orange lights along the windows and draped fake cobwebs in every corner. Dad helped us carve pumpkins, one for each of us. He carved Mom's while she supervised from her favorite chair, wrapped in a cozy blanket.

By Thursday, the house was almost ready, but we still had the ever crucial task of helping Scotty with his costume. He wanted to be Thunderbird, naturally. He was still obsessed with his favorite legend.

Emma came over to help transform Scotty's costume into a vibrant mix of colors, feathers, and faux fur, bringing her crafting expertise and hot glue gun.

"Okay, Thunderbird, let's see those wings," Emma said, unfolding a pair of magnificent wings we had constructed from wire and fabric.

Scotty's eyes widened as he tried them on, flapping around the living room, nearly knocking over a lamp in his excitement. "I'm gonna be the best Thunderbird ever!"

"You sure are," I said, laughing as I helped adjust his wings. "Let's add some more feathers here, for extra fierceness."

Over the weekend, we had a little pre-celebration with hot cocoa and Halloween movies. Scotty, in his Thunderbird costume, was practically vibrating with excitement.

"Can we watch 'Monster House'?" he asked, his eyes gleaming with anticipation.

"Only if you promise not to have nightmares," Dad teased, as he set up the movie, the flickering lights of the TV casting eerie shadows across the room.

As we all settled in, Mom resting with a warm blanket, Scotty wedged between Emma and me with Lucky on his lap, and Dad in his recliner, I felt a sense of togetherness that had been scarce lately. The laughter and warmth of my family, with my best friend there. It felt good to be all together like this. Since Zack had gone out of town with his mom for the weekend, Emma and I decided to have sleepovers each night, just like old times.

"Bring on Halloween," I whispered to myself, a smile tugging at my lips. The joy in the little moments, like Miss Torres said, they were here, in these shared times, these pockets of light amid the shadows.

And so, we were ready for Halloween, ready to embrace the spooky joy and the family memories it would bring. It was more than just a holiday; it was a night of escapism and fun, a night to be whoever we wanted to be, even if just for a few magical hours.

25

BROKEN STARS

Halloween night descended upon us, cloaking the neighborhood in a kaleidoscope of fantastical illusions. This year, however, the usual excitement was tinged with a somber undertone. With Zack working and Emma at a soccer league party, I found myself stepping into the role of Scotty's trick-or-treat guide. Our parents' grateful smiles lingered in my mind as Scotty and I ventured into the night.

The streets were alive with ghouls, witches, and an assortment of mythical beings, creating a world where reality and fantasy merged. I watched Scotty, his face alight with awe and excitement, proudly strutting up to each door as the confident Thunderbird. It was good to see him happy. He'd had a crease in his practically permanent furrowed brow these days, ever Mom's little worrier.

The night air was punctuated with the sounds of laughter and ghoulish music. Scotty's hand in mine felt small. It was in one of our quieter moments, under the vast, starry sky, that he posed the question that had been weighing on his young heart.

"V, do you think Mom is like the broken stars Thunderbird

takes care of?" His voice was barely above a whisper, a blend of curiosity and concern.

The question made me pause, and I knelt down to look into his earnest eyes, searching for a way to explain the inexplicable. "Scotty, Mom is like the bravest of stars. But even stars, as bright as they are, sometimes falter. It doesn't make them less brilliant, just more in need of our love."

"Is she going to break?" His eyes, wide and shimmering in the dim light, searched mine for an assurance I couldn't fully give.

Drawing him close, I felt the innocence and fear mingled in his question. "Mom is fighting with all her might, just like the bravest stars. We can't always fix everything, but we can be there, holding her hand, just like we're holding each other's hands right now."

Scotty leaned into the hug, his small body trembling. "Can we do something to help her not break?"

"Absolutely," I said, my voice laced with a mix of hope and melancholy. "We can make her a special get well card. We'll fill it with stars and all our love. It might not fix everything, but it will show her how much we care."

He nodded, a determined look crossing his face. "Let's make the best card ever, with the brightest stars!"

As we resumed our trick-or-treating, I saw a renewed vigor in Scotty. He darted from house to house, his laughter a bittersweet melody in the night air. Watching him, I felt a complex array of emotions—pride, love, and a piercing awareness of his fragile understanding of our reality.

The night drew to a close with a bag heavy with candy and hearts laden with unspoken fears and wishes. Back at home, seated at the kitchen table with colored papers, pencils, pens, glitter, and glue, Scotty and I poured our hearts into the get well card for Mom. Each star we drew was a silent prayer, a wish for healing, a symbol of our family's unyielding spirit.

As I tucked Scotty into bed, his eyelids heavy with the day's adventures, I whispered, "Your stars aren't broken; they're just learning how to shine brighter through the darkness."

With that, I turned off the light, leaving a sliver of moonlight to dance across his peaceful face. The night had been a journey of emotions, a reflection of our own story—a story of facing the unknown, of finding strength in our love, and of learning to navigate the darkness with the light of hope.

26

A DAY IN THE SUN

After saying goodnight to Scotty, I closed his bedroom door gently, using the dim glow of my phone to navigate the hallway. I paused for a moment, letting the stillness of the house wash over me, with Mom and Dad already in bed. The frenetic energy of trick-or-treating had faded, leaving behind a quiet that felt both comforting and lonely.

I got to my bedroom and leaned against the door, pulling out my phone. My fingers hovered above the screen, Zack's name bringing a bittersweet ache. His laughter now felt like a distant melody. With a deep breath, I tapped out a message, trying to sound light-hearted.

> Happy Halloween!🎃 Hope work isn't too boring. Scotty was adorable as Thunderbird. wish you could've seen him. We miss our Zee-man!🩶

I hit send before I could second-guess myself. It had been over two weeks since our last date, the Homecoming dance. I understood Zack's struggle with Amanda's loss, yet the growing distance between us was hard to ignore.

Resisting the urge to stare at my phone and wait for a reply, I tucked it away and headed downstairs. The kitchen area was a glittery aftermath of our earlier crafting. I swept up, each stroke of the broom a small distraction, though my mind kept drifting back to Zack. How he used to make me laugh with his ridiculous dance moves . . . nothing like his recent silence.

Then, my phone vibrated against my back pocket, jolting me back to the present. I fumbled to read the message, my heart racing:

A surprised laugh escaped my lips, my fingers typing a rapid, overjoyed response. Relief and excitement mingled in my chest. Maybe this was the start of a new chapter for us, where smiles weren't as rare.

I clutched the phone to my chest, a silly grin spreading across my face. For the first time in weeks, I felt a flutter of hope, like the first warm breeze of spring after a long, cold winter. I slept better that night than I had in a long time, dreams filled with sandy beaches and laughter.

And Saturday couldn't get here fast enough.

★ ★ ★ ★ ★

THE SATURDAY SUN was already high in the sky, pouring its warmth over the golden sands as Zack and I arrived at the beach. The ocean stretched out before us, a dazzling blue canvas sprinkled with surfers. I felt a lightness in my chest, a freedom from all the shadows that had been with us lately.

Zack parked his black Nissan Pathfinder near a cluster of palms, the sound of the waves harmonizing with the music. He jumped out, his smile as bright as the day, and came around to open my door. "Ready for an epic beach day?" he asked, his hand extended toward me.

I took his hand, feeling the familiar warmth of his grip. "Absolutely," I replied, my heart skipping with excitement.

We found a perfect spot, not too far from the water, where the sand was warm and inviting. Zack spread out two large, colorful beach towels and I unpacked our picnic basket, filled with sandwiches, chips, and cold lemonade. He kicked off his flip flops and raced toward the waves, beckoning me to follow. I laughed and chased after him, the sand giving way under my feet.

The beach was our playground, the cool water our stage as Zack and I engaged in an impromptu splash war. The ocean's chill was a shock at first, but I adjusted quickly, the playful skirmish heating things up. Our laughter was a natural soundtrack, blending with the rhythmic crash of the waves. In a spontaneous moment, Zack scooped me up, spinning me around before pulling me into a breath-stealing kiss. In that instant, it felt like we were the only two souls on Earth.

Later, we were architects, constructing a sandcastle that was more whimsical than structurally sound. Zack crowned us king and queen of our lopsided domain. It wasn't going to win any awards, but it was ours, and in that moment, it was perfect. We sat shoulder to shoulder, surveying our sandy kingdom with a sense of pride.

Lunch was laidback—just us on our towels, stretching out under the sun. The sandwiches were simple, our fingers sticky with salt and chips. Zack elbowed me playfully, his eyes sparkling with a challenge. "Race you to the shoreline," he declared.

"You're on!" I leaped up, and we raced across the sand, our laughter echoing behind us. I claimed victory, though Zack later joked he'd been distracted by a seagull.

As the day wore on, the sun began its slow descent, casting long shadows over the beach. We lay back, hands entwined, watching the clouds meander across the sky. Words were unnecessary; the silence between us was comfortable, complete.

Lying there, with the gentle cadence of the waves and Zack's steady breathing beside me, I found a rare sense of tranquility. All the worries—my mom's illness, the loss Zack had endured, the everyday struggles—they all seemed to drift away, carried off by the ocean breeze. It was just Zack and me, two kids in love, cocooned in our perfect beach day.

As twilight painted the sky in shades of violet and orange, Zack turned to me, his eyes reflecting the sunset. "Today was perfect," he whispered.

I snuggled closer, watching day turn to dusk. "The best day," I agreed, keenly aware of how precious these moments of untroubled joy were.

The beach had quieted down as we packed up, the only sounds our footsteps and the waves' soft caress. Walking back to his car, it felt like we were floating, our hearts light, carrying with us the memory of a day where everything was just as it should be—a flawless moment in time.

<h1 style="text-align:center">27</h1>

<h2 style="text-align:center">THIS IS NOT A DRILL</h2>

After our idyllic day at the beach, Zack and I were riding a high that made the rest of the week feel like a breeze. But come Friday, reality crashed back in, as mundane as any other school day. That is until fifth period AP Physics, when we met our substitute, Mrs. Proxy. She looked kind enough but had this air of being a bit out of her depth.

The class, a motley crew of brainiacs from various grades, had just settled down when the lockdown alarm cut through the air, a sound that chilled to the bone. This was no drill. Tension rippled through the room like a live wire.

The shrill ring of the phone on Mrs. Proxy's desk shattered the uneasy silence. She picked up the receiver, her hand shaking. The look on her face as she hung up mirrored the anxiety buzzing through all of us. "The office says we're to stay put and wait." Her voice was thin, brittle, like she was on the edge of breaking.

My eyes scanned the classroom. The physics posters on the walls felt like silent, helpless onlookers. Mrs. Proxy's gaze was locked on the large window, a glaring vulnerability. We were sitting ducks, second floor, no easy escape, no place to hide.

"Should we get under the desks?" someone asked, breaking the tense quiet.

Mrs. Proxy nodded, her voice a tremulous echo. "Yes, yes, that's a good idea. Under your desks, everyone, now."

We all dove under our desks, a drill turned into stark reality. The room was filled with quiet sobs and the frantic clicking of texts being sent. My heart was hammering against my ribs, the unknown whereabouts of the shooter casting a dark shadow over us.

The phone rang again, making us all jump. Mrs. Proxy answered, her expression unreadable. "It's my first day subbing," she half-joked, half-sobbed. "I don't have email, so they call here." She took a deep breath, steadying herself. "They've informed me the shooter has fled the building. He's now in the neighborhood, and the police are chasing him. We're not in immediate danger. You can come out now and return to your seats."

We emerged, letting out a collective sigh of relief. But my gut still felt uneasy. I remained guarded.

The lockdown eventually lifted, and we shuffled to our last class of the day. In Art, where seniors went for an easy credit, the vibe was jarringly different. Laughter, jokes, indifference— it was like they were untouched by the scare. Shane came in, fresh from the office gossip mill. "It was some freshman," he spilled, and the class erupted in a flurry of social media sleuthing.

"Ugh, that guy's ugly," sneered one student.

Another joined in. "Yeah, saw him around. Always walked funny." He stood up, imitating the walk to a chorus of laughs. "Why'd he bring a gun, though?"

I snapped. "Maybe because of jerks like you!" The room fell silent. "He was probably sick of being pushed around and decided to push back."

As school let out, my mind lingered on the shooter. A kid, just like us, but so lost. What now for him? The casual cruelty of my classmates left a bitter taste in my mouth, a grim reminder of the empathy and understanding so often missing in our halls.

LATER, the details of the day's chaos trickled down to us. Two shots fired into the dirt at the softball fields, the shooter pinpointed by a couple of eagle-eyed witnesses, and nabbed by the cops in some neighborhood off campus.

But the email from our principal, Dr. Michael Fitzgibbon, to our parents was like reading about a completely different event. It was all calm, clinical—a stark contrast to the fear, the frenzy, and the whirlwind of emotions we'd all been thrown into. The email on my phone felt like it was whitewashing the day's events, turning our ordeal into a sanitized, bureaucratic blip.

Sitting in my room, the day's events still swirling in my head, I read:

"Dear Sierra Families,

I want to inform you about a lockdown incident at our school today. Our campus was temporarily placed on lockdown by the Orange County Sheriff's Office due to a report of an incident in the area. The lockdown was in place for 50 minutes and was lifted as soon as we got the all-clear from law enforcement.

I want to assure you that our students were never in any real danger. The lockdown was simply a precaution, a joint decision by our local law enforcement and school staff. Please know that we always treat these situations with the utmost seriousness, and the safety of our students is our foremost concern.

Dr. Michael Fitzgibbon

Principal, Sierra High School"

The email's formal, detached tone was like a cold slap, a sharp contrast to the raw terror we'd experienced. I remembered Mrs. Proxy's wide, frightened eyes, the muffled cries from under desks, the adrenaline-fueled fear coursing through us. None of that was captured in these dry, sanitized sentences.

My dad knocked softly and opened my door. His face, usually calm, bore subtle traces of the day's strain. As a history teacher at Sierra High, he wasn't just my dad today; he was an educator who had lived through the same lockdown.

"You saw Michael's—your principal's—email?" he asked, taking a seat on my bed.

"Yeah, it reads like it's about some other school," I said, my voice tinged with bitterness.

He nodded, a hint of agreement in his eyes. "It's . . . clinical. That's how these communications are. As teachers, we're trained to stay calm, to keep you safe."

"But it wasn't calm, Dad. We were terrified. It feels like they're missing the point," I argued, my frustration bubbling to the surface.

He sighed, a tired hand running through his hair. "Fear is

part of it, yes. But in our roles, your mom's and mine, we have to provide a stable front. Even when we're scared too."

"I'm glad Mom wasn't there today."

His smile was faint, tinged with sadness. "Your mom would've been just as strong. We all try to be, for you kids. But it doesn't mean we're unaffected."

I pondered his words. Being a student in a lockdown was one thing; being a teacher, responsible for those students, was something else entirely. Their courage was an unsung, often overlooked, armor.

As Dad got up to leave, he stopped, his gaze thoughtful. "In history, we learn from the past to better the future. This . . . will be part of your history, a lesson for us all."

His words lingered in the air as he left. I looked at the email again, but this time through a different lens. I wasn't just a student in the midst of chaos; I was the daughter of educators who had to juggle their own fears with the duty of safeguarding their students. It was a delicate, emotionally charged balance, one that couldn't be captured in the sterile lines of an official email.

28

SEASON OF CHANGE

In the shadow of the school shooter scare, time seemed to warp. Days blurred into weeks, each tinted with a surreal quality, as if I was living in some prolonged, uneasy dream. Every unexpected sound made me jump, reminding me of the deep-rooted scars the incident left behind. It's one thing to see stories about school shootings on the news; it's a whole other beast to live through that terror in your own backyard. My school, once a sanctuary, now felt like a glass house—fragile and transparent.

Mom went back to work the following Monday, but only part-time, three days a week. I had mixed emotions about her return. Part of me wanted to cocoon her from the world, to keep her safe and sound at home. But there she was, steadfast as ever, insisting, "My kids need me." Her conviction was both a source of worry and awe for me. Then she'd crack a joke. "Don't they know not to mess with a redhead?" And I'd find myself smiling despite the tension.

As autumn faded into winter, life found its rhythm again. Thanksgiving arrived, its warmth infused with a deeper sense of gratitude and introspection. Finals rushed by in a blur of textbooks and caffeine-fueled study sessions with Zack and Emma, the nights stretching into marathons of memorization and last-minute cramming.

Life was slowly edging back to normal, or at least our new version of it. But the echoes of that day in the school corridors lingered, a subtle undercurrent in the back of my mind, a reminder that normal was just a fragile, fleeting illusion.

Christmas glowed with an extra layer of meaning this year. Our family gatherings, brimming with laughter and stories, felt like a warm embrace enveloping us all—moments to be cherished. Watching my parents celebrate their 18th anniversary, I saw a love that seemed almost otherworldly in its depth, a kind of magic that seemed to defy the odds.

The winter break unfolded quietly. With Emma and her mom off exploring college prospects and Zack buried in work, solitude became my unexpected sidekick. I retreated into the world of books and music, finding solace in their timeless comfort. Yet, by the time school swung back into session, I felt a strange mix of readiness and apprehension. The hallways were the same, but something in me had shifted. It was like walking back onto a stage where the script had been rewritten, where the ghosts of yesterday lingered just out of sight. School wasn't just a place of learning anymore; it was a landscape changed, a reminder of life's unpredictable turns.

RAINDROPS TRACED melancholy paths down my bedroom window. It was the rainy season here, which lasted about two to three weeks so I had no right to complain. A true Californian, I took our usual sunny days for granted. I watched the rain, lost in thought when my phone's buzz got my attention. It was from Emma, her text breaking the gloomy spell of the rain.

> Guess what?! UNC-Chapel Hill offered me a full-ride soccer scholarship!!!!

Her words leapt off the screen, full of excitement.

> Emma, that's amazing! Congratulations!!

I typed back, genuinely happy for her.

> The head coach himself personally extended the UNC promise!

> Promise?

> It's a verbal offer or promise since I'm being recruited early. Obviously, I won't get the actual scholarship for a while.

I was about to ask her more questions when another message popped up.

> Sorry to cut this short but I gotta go. Tell u all about it when u pick us up at the airport, k?

> K. Have a great time. Miss you!

> Miss u too!

I set my phone aside and returned my gaze to the window. The rain seemed a bit less gloomy now. Emma and I had taken different paths in life—I, far from athletic, always felt more at home in a world of books and music. But our friendship had weathered all changes, growing stronger despite our differences.

As the rain tapped a rhythmic beat against the window pane, I realized how much Emma's news meant. It was a new chapter for her, a giant leap forward into a future she'd often dreamed about. I just wished that dream didn't have to take her to a school so far away from me.

I shook it off, reminding myself it was a season of change all around. After all, Zack's news was just as life-altering.

ZACK'S BLAST from the past, Malia Kahale, had suddenly resurfaced from Hawaii, and the real kicker was I only heard about it through the gossip of social media. Zack—my boyfriend—hadn't breathed a word, until now.

We were sitting in his car, parked in my driveway after a date that felt more like we were going through the motions. Zack had been off lately, and I was about at my limit. "Zack, what's going on? Are we good?" I had to confront him.

He looked genuinely puzzled. "Why wouldn't we be? What's up?"

I fixed him with a look, my arms crossed in front of me.

He shifted uncomfortably, avoiding my eyes. "Just . . . school, work. You know, the usual stress."

I wasn't buying it. "No, it's more than that. You've been distant. Like you're hiding something. Spill."

"Nothing's going on," he protested.

"So who's been lighting up your phone recently? And why do you go all secret agent every time I see you texting?" I challenged, feeling hurt and suspicious. "Don't you trust me?"

He reached for my hand, his face a mix of guilt and frustration. "V, I do trust you. It's just . . . complicated."

"Try me."

He sighed, looking like he was about to confess to a crime. "Malia Kahale. She's back in town."

"Your childhood best friend? Skater girl from Hawaii?"

"Yeah, that's the one."

"And you're into her?" My voice was barely above a whisper, bracing for the worst.

"No! It's not like that. I knew you'd freak out. That's why I didn't want to tell you."

I lied through my teeth. "I'm not freaking out. I just want to know why you're acting like a guy in a spy novel."

"Well . . . Malia and I, we go way back. But that's all in the past. I didn't want to make a big deal out of nothing."

His words should have reassured me, but doubt was already doing its dance in my head. "You should've just been honest with me from the beginning," I said, my voice a quiet accusation.

He nodded, full of regret. "You're right. I should've. And, V?"

I braced myself. "What now?"

"I got her a job at Skaterz."

"You what? Is that why you're always at work? Cozying up to Malia?"

He rushed to explain. "No! We've been slammed with end-of-year inventory. It's all hands on deck. Malia working there has nothing to do with it. I just wanted to come clean, no more secrets. You're everything to me, V. I can't lose you over this."

The porch light flicked on, my dad's voice cutting through the tension. "V? It's time to call it a night."

"Okay, Dad. I'll be right there," I called back. "Zack, we'll pick this up later, okay?"

"Sure. Anything you want to know, I'm an open book."

I gave him a quick hug and a kiss on the cheek, making sure it looked good for any parental eyes, then bolted from the car. As I hurried into the house, I didn't look back, my mind a whirlwind of doubts and uneasy thoughts.

29

HOLIDAY HOPES AND SOCCER DREAMS

The New Year's Day sun cast a warm, golden glow over LAX as I pulled over to the curb at the airport pickup zone to wait. Today was the day Emma and her mom, Rosa, were returning from their visit to UNC-Chapel Hill.

The crowd ebbed and flowed around me, a sea of reunions and farewells. At last, I spotted them. Emma's brown eyes were alight with a brilliance I hadn't seen before, and Rosa, ever the supportive mother, had an arm wrapped affectionately around her daughter's shoulders.

I hopped out of my Subaru to help them with their luggage.

"V!" Emma exclaimed, dropping her bag and pulling me into a tight hug. "I've missed you so much!"

"Missed you too," I said, my voice muffled in her shoulder. Stepping back, I turned to her mom. "Welcome back, Rosa."

Rosa's warm smile was comforting. "Thank you, V. It's good to be back, though the trip was wonderful."

Luggage loaded into the back, we were on our way, navigating the busy Los Angeles traffic.

"Thank you for picking us up, V," Rosa said, good-naturedly taking the backseat so Emma and I could talk.

"It was my pleasure," I replied. "Now tell me all about your trip."

Emma launched into her story, her hands gesturing animatedly. "The campus is so beautiful! Like something out of a movie. And the soccer facilities are top-notch!"

Rosa nodded, her eyes reflecting pride. "And the head coach is so impressive. He personally extended the scholarship offer to Emma."

I glanced at Emma. "So, a full ride, right? That's incredible, Em."

Emma beamed, a flush of pride coloring her cheeks. "Yeah, it's a dream come true. I still can't believe it."

As we merged onto the highway, heading toward Orange, the conversation ebbed into comfortable silence. The skyline of Los Angeles receded in the mirror, giving way to the familiar sprawl of the surrounding suburbs.

Breaking the silence, Rosa spoke to Emma. "Mija, your father would be so proud of you."

Emma's smile softened, a hint of sadness in her eyes. "I hope so, Mama."

The mention of Emma's dad, who had died a few months after she was born, brought a bittersweet note to the conversation. He would have been Emma's biggest fan, an avid soccer player in his youth.

I cleared my throat, steering the conversation back to safer waters. "So, when do you start at UNC?"

Emma's excitement returned in full force. "Fall 2019. Can you believe it? I'll be playing soccer at one of the best programs in the country!"

I smiled but felt a pang of sadness. "I'm going to miss you like crazy, you know."

"I know, V. And I'll miss you, too. But it's two years away. We've got time."

I nodded, trying to mask the sadness that threatened to spill over. "I know, but it won't be the same without you."

She placed her hand on my knee. "We've got plenty of time left together. And hey, who knows? Maybe by then, I'll talk you into going to UNC with me." A mischievous smile played on her lips.

I couldn't help but laugh, despite the ache in my heart. "Yeah, right. Me, at UNC? In your dreams, soccer star."

We reached Emma's house just as the sun was setting, painting the sky in vivid colors. I helped them unload their luggage, trying not to look sad.

"Hey," Emma said as she hugged me goodbye, "think about it, okay? I'm serious about you coming to UNC with me. We'd be unstoppable together."

I forced a smile, my heart heavy. "I'll think about it," I promised.

Emma's words echoed in my mind as I drove home. The possibility of attending UNC-Chapel Hill, a place so different from here had never crossed my mind. Honestly, I hadn't really thought about where I wanted to go for college at all. I just always knew that I would go—somewhere.

Yet, the idea of being part of Emma's journey, of not letting distance grow between us, was tempting. Did I have the courage to step out of my comfort zone, to chase a dream that wasn't entirely mine?

30

NEW YEAR, NEW PROBLEMS

There are times I wonder if the big guy upstairs has a bit of a twisted sense of humor, and this was definitely one of those moments. It felt like the universe was playing some kind of cosmic joke on me. As if Zack keeping Malia's return and her new job at Skaterz a secret wasn't enough, she had to go and enroll at my school too.

Walking into fourth-period Psychology on our first day back from winter break, there she was—Malia, standing next to Ms. Yang's desk like she owned the place. Zack's description of her as 'plain' was a gross understatement. The girl was a knockout, straight-up gorgeous. She was like a walking, talking embodiment of Hawaii—sun-kissed skin that glowed like she was perpetually basking in a tropical sunset, hair that flowed like it was always riding a gentle ocean breeze, and eyes that seemed to hold the depth of the Pacific.

As I gawked, probably a bit too obviously, she headed my way. Great, just great. She recognized me. Extending her hand, she hit me with, "Aloha, V. Zack's told me so much about you! I'm Malia. Really excited to finally meet you. Hope we can be friends." She flashed a smile that could light up the darkest room, her teeth annoyingly perfect.

Her words hung there, suspended in the air, as I mechanically placed my hand in hers. My own smile felt forced, artificial. Was she genuinely this friendly, or was it all an act? Doubt and a dash of paranoia nipped at my heels. Trying to keep my cool, I managed to say through a tight smile, "Nice to meet you, Malia. Funny, Zack hasn't really mentioned you."

TWO DAYS LATER, I pulled a surprise visit on Zack at Skaterz. It'd been a while since I'd visited him at work, and I needed to see the 'Mack and Zack team' in action.

The shop's bell jingled as I stepped in, a sound that used to feel welcoming. Today, though, it was like the opening note of a suspenseful soundtrack, my stomach tying itself in knots.

Skaterz was a visual explosion of skateboards and accessories, the air thick with the scent of new rubber and varnish. I expected to find Zack charming the socks off customers or manning the register. Instead, there he was with Malia, both laughing over a display of skate shoes. My heart took a nosedive.

I hung back for a moment, watching them. Zack's laughter was just a bit too loud, his grin a touch too bright. Malia seemed right at home, her tomboy style clashing with her natural grace, wearing a backward ball cap. Seeing them together, so comfortable and familiar, set off a flare of jealousy in me.

I took a deep breath and approached them, my footsteps

lost in the shop's carpet. Zack's face broke into a genuine smile. "V! Didn't expect you. What's up?"

"Just checking in," I said, a smile plastered on my face. "It's been a while since I last stopped by." Malia gave a casual wave, and I nodded back, our exchange an awkward dance of pleasantries.

"Hey, V," Malia greeted, her tone friendly but cautious. There was an unspoken tension between us, a silent acknowledgement of the weird triangle we found ourselves in.

Zack was blissfully ignorant of the undercurrents. "Malia's been awesome around here, knows her stuff," he said, his voice held a hint of pride.

"That's . . . nice," I said, feeling like a third wheel. Watching them, the ease of their interaction just reminded me of their shared history.

Malia excused herself to attend to a customer, leaving Zack and me alone. "So, what's really going on, V?" he leaned on the counter, his face questioning.

I hesitated, suddenly unsure of my script. "Just wanted to see you. But you look busy," I said, the edge in my voice unmistakable.

Zack caught the bitterness. "Is something wrong? You seem . . . off."

I looked away, torn between opening up and playing it cool. "It's just . . . seeing you and Malia together. It's hard," I admitted, meeting his eyes again.

He reached out, his touch meant to reassure me. "V, you know she's just a friend, right? You're my priority."

I wanted to believe him, to trust in the strength of our relationship. But the unease Malia's return stirred was hard to ignore. "I know, it's just . . . ." I trailed off, my voice fading.

Zack nodded, his expression softening. "I get it. But trust me, there's nothing to worry about."

We made small talk for a bit before I left, claiming errands. As I left Skaterz, the sound of their laughter followed me, a haunting reminder of the complicated mess I was in.

The drive home was a blur of conflicting emotions. Part of me wanted to trust Zack, to believe his words. But there was another part, a nagging voice whispering doubts every time I pictured him with Malia.

As I parked in front of my house, it hit me. This was about more than just about Malia. It was about trust, about a relationship being stretched and tested in ways I never saw coming.

WHEN I GOT HOME, I let out a sigh that felt like it carried the weight of the world.

"Violet, is that you?" Mom's voice, weaker now, floated from the living room.

"Yeah, Mom, it's me," I called back, nostalgia hitting me as she used my full name. Ever since I'd rebranded myself as 'V' two years ago, hearing 'Violet' had become a rarity. I enjoyed hearing my mom say it. Dropping my backpack, I headed to where she was, cocooned in a cozy blanket on the couch.

Mom had always been a force of nature, but cancer had whittled her down, leaving a delicate version of the power-house I grew up with. Her smile, though, remained unchanged —warm and comforting, despite everything.

"How was school?" she asked, her eyes searching mine, looking for any sign of the day's battles.

"It was okay," I lied, forcing a smile. "You know, the usual."

She nodded, her gaze drifting to the window where the day's last light faded away. "I got some news today, Violet. I've been approved for disability retirement. I'm going to focus on getting better, on beating this."

I sat down beside her and took her frail hand in mine. It felt cold. "That's good, Mom. You need to rest."

She squeezed my hand, a silent thanks. "I know it's going to be tough, but we'll get through this, right? We're a team."

"Absolutely," I said, my voice stronger than I felt. Inside, I was a mess. The reality of her illness, the uphill battle she faced, it was overwhelming. But I had to be her rock, like she'd always been mine.

Our conversation drifted to lighter topics: a new recipe she wanted to try, some upcoming school events. But the elephant in the room, her illness, lurked in the background, an uninvited presence at our mother-daughter duo.

After a while, I retreated to my room, craving solitude, a place to process. My desk was cluttered with notes and textbooks, reminding me of the essay due tomorrow. But my focus shifted to my investigation—Jacob and his crew. This case had become my lifeline, a distraction from the all-consuming reality of Mom's cancer.

I dove into the clues, piecing together the puzzle. Here, in this detective world, I was in control. I needed something to counteract the helplessness I felt with Mom's situation.

Hours passed, and I worked relentlessly, the case a welcome escape from the fear and uncertainty that had taken up residence in my life.

Exhausted, I finally crawled into bed, the events of the past days replaying in my mind. A new year, with new problems. As I drifted off to sleep, a quote I'd read recently came to mind,

"Life is not about waiting for the storm to pass. It's about learning how to dance in the rain."

And dance I would, through every challenge, every setback. Because that's what we did in our family. We faced things head-on, together. Tomorrow was another day, another piece of the puzzle to fit into place. And I was ready for it, whatever it threw my way.

31
A CHAPTER ENDS AND ANOTHER BEGINS

The next day began with a sense of finality, a turning of the page in the story of our lives. As I logged onto the school's online newsletter, the words of our principal stood out vividly, announcing Mom's decision to the entire school community. She would take the rest of the academic year off to focus on her battle with cancer. The words on the screen blurred as I read and re-read the announcement, each word sinking in deeper.

"Nearly two and a half years ago, Mrs. Jiménez was diagnosed with Stage 4 breast cancer. She bravely faced this challenge in a very public battle, serving as a representative for UCI Medical Center and the Orange Fire Department's efforts to find cancer cures. Mrs. Jiménez successfully overcame the disease and rejoined us at Sierra High, where her return was celebrated. She is a valuable and extraordinary member of our family, and her presence is immensely appreciated.

However, the disease has resurfaced, posing as great a challenge as before. To conquer this battle, Mrs. Jiménez is dedicating herself to fighting the cancer full-time, necessitating her absence for the remainder of the school year. She needs our unwavering support as we rally behind her once again, hopeful to defeat this terrible disease for a second time. Upon her victory, which we anticipate eagerly, Mrs. Jiménez plans to return to Sierra. Cancer will not define Hannah Jiménez; it will not rob us of who she is. The battle ahead is daunting, yet our thoughts, prayers, and support are with Mrs. Hannah Jiménez! Together, we will once again 'Fight Warrior Strong!'

—Dr. Michael Fitzgibbon

The school staff organized a surprise retirement party for her at lunchtime. It wasn't really a retirement, not officially, but it felt like it in so many ways. The uncertainty of her return hung in the air like an unspoken question. Would she go back? Nobody seemed to have an answer, not even Mom.

At dinner that night, Mom told us about the party, her eyes sparkling with a mixture of joy and sadness. "It was lovely," she began, "the staff room was decorated with streamers and a huge banner, 'To Our Brave Hannah.' It's hard to imagine I've been there for twenty years. I still remember when I was a student teacher."

"Tell the kids about your impromptu speech," Dad prompted.

Mom laughed. "You mean the part where I overshared and talked too long? Well, okay, if you insist."

We all laughed.

"Was there cake?" Scotty asked.

"You bet there was, sweetie. It was a delicious chocolate cake with chocolate frosting. You would have loved it."

"Is there any cake left over?"

"Sorry, no. My co-workers ate it all. Can you believe it?"

"Yes, teachers love cake!" Scotty said, a self-satisfied smirk on his face.

"So . . .," I reminded her, "the speech?"

"Oh! Well, I can't remember exactly what I said. It was off-the-cuff, you know? It's just . . . the entire event. It was such a beautiful celebration. And so many people were there, too, not just teachers, but the office staff, cafeteria workers, some volunteer parents. It's hard to explain, but those thirty minutes filled my soul. I embraced the moment. I embraced all the love and support and people in the room. I embraced the acknowledgment of my career. That party was a defining moment in my life. And I'll never be able to truly thank everyone enough."

"You had everyone in that room crying," Dad teased her. "But it's only because they all love you so much. You have made such an incredible impact at our school. The students come up to me daily and tell me how much of a difference you've made in their lives, things that go beyond the curriculum you taught them. You cared about them. You were kind. And your simple words, comments, and actions did not go unnoticed. The kids you've helped over the years will remember you, for the rest of their lives."

Mom was crying again. "Oh yeah?" she said, playfully. "It takes one to know one, Mr. J. Kids, you know I met your father my first year at Sierra, right?"

Scotty and I both nodded. "Yes, Mom, we know."

Unfazed, she continued, "And if anyone was born to be a teacher, it is your dad. I'm just so thankful that I was the lucky girl who got to marry him! Carlos has shown me what teaching is all about. He has been my role model in every way."

"Hannah, darling, don't make this about me. Today was your day." Dad said, gazing lovingly at Mom. "You're the real super hero at this table. Besides, when I asked you to tell the kids about your speech, I actually meant that line you said. It cracked me up."

"What line?"

"About being a woman of leisure now."

"Oh, that line." They laughed. "Well, it's true."

When she said that, I thought about what it meant for us as a family. Having Mom home all the time would be an adjustment. Part of me was relieved she'd be resting, but another part was scared about what her being home signified. It was a reminder of the battle she still faced.

But if there was one thing I knew about my mom, it was her tenacity and her ability to find joy in the smallest things. Her strength and positivity were inspiring, even in adversity.

Sitting there with my family, talking about Mom's party and what the future might hold, I knew this wasn't just an end, it was also a beginning. It was a new chapter in our lives, one we would navigate together—with love, courage, and our unbreakable family bond.

32
WHISPERS OF DOUBTS

onday kicked off like any other day until lunchtime rolled around, flipping me inside out. Emma and I, perched at our usual table, were doing our thing—unwrapping homemade sandwiches and chatting about UNC, peppered with my not-so-subtle ribbing about her ditching me. Then, everything changed.

Zack showed up with Malia, crashing our lunchtime bubble. "Hey, mind if Malia joins us?" he asked, all smiles and casual charm.

Emma's eyes lit up with a mischievous glint. "So this is the infamous Mack . . . the other half of the 'Mack and Zack' legacy," she teased, her words dancing with curiosity.

I shot her a warning glance, a silent signal to ease off.

Malia was momentarily thrown. "Infamous? What's that about?"

Emma, realizing she might've stepped into a minefield, backpedaled. "Just, you know, your skateboarding skills are kind of a big deal here."

Malia laughed it off, too effortlessly. "That? Ancient history.

But yeah, Zack's the only one who still calls me Mack." She gave Zack a playful nudge, a move that was a little too close for comfort.

I felt a knot of annoyance tighten in my stomach. Their easy banter, her casual touch. It was like watching a well-rehearsed play where everyone knew their lines but me.

Zack, clueless, chimed in with his usual nonchalance. "You guys gonna make room for us, or what?"

I reluctantly shuffled over, my backpack hitting the ground with a thud. The round table, designed for equal opportunity seating, suddenly felt lopsided.

We ate in strained silence for a bit, punctuated by Zack and Malia's shared laughter and inside jokes. Watching them, I felt like an outsider peeking into a world I wasn't part of.

Emma, ever the icebreaker, asked Malia about being back. "So, Malia, how does it feel being home again? Did you miss it?"

Malia smiled softly. "It's definitely a change, for sure. But this isn't home, and it's only temporary." She looked at Zack before continuing, "I was born in Hawaii, on the island of Kauai. But when I turned six, my dad's company moved us to Los Angeles, where I attended first grade. That's when Zack and I met." She nabbed a French fry off his tray.

I jumped in, trying to keep myself in the loop. "I've been to Hawaii. I visited the Big Island with my family when I was ten. We loved it. My mom fell in love with the volcanos and lava flows. In fact, she said when she dies she wants her ashes scattered there."

The table went dead silent, everyone staring at me.

"I mean, not now! Like, way in the future," I hastily added.

"So, Malia, what do you mean this is just a temporary move?" Emma asked, steering the conversation back on track.

Malia hesitated, glancing at Zack.

He nodded, encouraging her.

"The company my dad works for is headquartered in San Francisco. They have offices all over, and they send my dad to different cities to train their employees. He's only here two months, then his new base will be in San Francisco. I'll finish out the semester here, then Mom and I will join Dad as soon as the school year's over."

Zack beamed. "It's great having Malia back, even if only for a little while. We used to have epic adventures as kids." His eyes sparkled with nostalgia, and something inside me twisted uncomfortably, but knowing Malia wouldn't be here very long gave me hope.

"We should hang out some time," Emma said. "Show Malia some of our favorite spots."

"Yeah, that'd be great," Zack said enthusiastically, then shot a quick glance my way, but I couldn't read his expression.

I mustered a smile, feeling like an outsider in my own circle. "Yeah, sounds great," I said, but the words tasted like cardboard.

Malia caught my vibe. "Only if V's cool with it. I don't want to intrude. After all, I'm the new person here."

Her gaze held mine, curiosity and something unreadable. Was it sincerity or just a good act? "No, it's all good. We're all friends here," I lied.

The rest of lunch continued with light forced chatter. Inside, I was a mess. Each laugh, each shared memory between Zack and Malia chipped away at my composure. I couldn't shake the feeling that I was witnessing the slow unraveling of my world.

THE UNEASE I'd felt during lunch clung to me like a shadow as I slipped into AP Physics. Under the desk, I fired off a text to Zack. I needed some kind of clarity, something to anchor me in this sea of doubt.

> Can we talk after school? It's important.

The reply came too swiftly,

> Can't, babe. Work's slammed.

I frowned at my phone.

> But you're always at work. It feels like you're a ghost in my life now.

His text was curt, a digital brush-off.

> You know the shop's crazy busy this time of year. But I can do 10 min. After school. K?

> Fine. See you at your car.

I slipped my phone back into my backpack before Mrs. Rodriguez caught me. The rest of the day dragged like a bad movie, each second stretching out torturously. By the time Art class wrapped up, my thoughts were a tornado of worry and frustration. I rushed out, barely acknowledging Emma's puzzled look, and headed straight for Zack's Pathfinder in the student lot.

Zack showed up, his walk confident yet exhausted. We hopped into his car, the space suddenly too close, too charged.

"So, what's up?" he asked, a hint of impatience in his voice.

I hesitated, the words tangling in my throat. "At lunch today, Malia said she's moving to San Francisco at the end of the semester."

"And?" He seemed genuinely confused.

"It's just . . . you two seemed pretty cozy, and I can't help but wonder if . . ." My voice faltered, fear threading through every word.

Zack's face softened, but his eyes wouldn't meet mine. "What are you getting at, V?"

I swallowed the lump in my throat. "Are you into her, Zack? Like, more than just friends? Like, will you leave me?"

He turned to me, his face a mask of disbelief. "V, seriously? Come on, you know that's not going to happen. I'm with you, aren't I? And Malia's moving away in a few months, so why would I . . ."

"But that's not what I asked, Zack." My voice was firmer now, demanding. "Do you have feelings for her?"

There was a pause, a heavy silence that felt like a verdict. "You're overthinking this, V. I'm with you. That's what matters, right?"

His words were meant to reassure me, but they fell flat. He leaned in for a kiss, a brief touch that lacked its usual warmth. I reciprocated out of habit, then stepped out of the car, the cool air echoing the chill settling in my heart.

As I watched his car disappear, the unspoken words hung heavy in the air. He hadn't really answered my question. And in that silence—the things left unsaid—my doubts found fertile ground to grow.

33

HAPPY ANNIVERSARY?

Standing in front of the mirror, I adjusted the silver heart necklace Zack gave me for our six-month mark. Tonight was supposed to be special—one year since Zack and I had our first date, a study session at the library for an AP Euro test. The next night, after we aced the test, he took me on a proper date. A year since he stopped being 'Crash' and started being 'Zack' in my life. All week, I'd been caught up in a daydream, wondering what romantic plans he might have up his sleeve for tonight.

As I applied a final touch of gloss to my lips, my phone buzzed. It was a text from Zack:

Outside. Ready?

My heart did a little skip. I grabbed my purse, gave myself a last look in the mirror, and hurried outside. The evening air was a cool caress against my skin. Zack was there, casual as ever, leaning against his car, phone in hand. His greeting was lukewarm. "Hey, V."

"Hey!" I tried to sound upbeat, but my heart sank at the lack of excitement in his voice. "What's the plan?"

Zack shrugged. "Thought we'd catch a movie. 'Explosive Retribution' is playing. Heard it's good," he said, nonchalantly.

An action flick? Not exactly the romantic evening I had envisioned. "Sounds . . . exhilarating," I said, my voice betraying my disappointment.

The drive to the theater was filled with the kind of small talk that made the silence seem loud. The usual spark between us felt like it was on a dimmer switch, turned down low. I wondered if Zack even knew the special significance of this date.

At the theater, Zack did the usual, tickets and popcorn, but the whole thing felt mechanical. Once we settled into our seats, I was struck by how alone I felt. As the lights dimmed and the trailers began, Zack's attention was riveted to the screen, more excited with every explosion and fight scene. I, on the other hand, felt like a spectator in my own anniversary.

Halfway through the movie, I reached for his hand, craving some connection. He squeezed it, but the gesture felt obligatory. Soon, he was back to being absorbed in the unfolding action on the screen. He withdrew his hand to get more popcorn and never put it back; a lump formed in my throat.

When the movie ended, we walked back to the car, shrouded in a silence that felt heavy. I kept hoping the night would take a turn, that maybe he'd surprise me. But the ride home was just a blur of streetlights and unspoken words.

Pulling up outside my house, Zack turned to me, his expression apologetic. But his apology was like a verbal band-aid. "Got work early. You get it, right?"

I nodded, masking my hurt. "Sure, work's important."

His goodbye kiss was quick, impersonal. "Thanks for understanding, V. I'll text you."

Watching his car fade into the night, I was engulfed in a wave of sadness. This was not how I imagined our first anniversary. The lack of effort, the missing spark—it all felt wrong. It was a far cry from the love-filled beginning we had.

Walking inside, I ignored my family in the living room and headed straight to my room, closing the door behind me. I kicked off my shoes, collapsed onto my bed, and didn't know whether to laugh or cry. Tonight didn't even seem real. It was like a badly written scene in a Rom-Com. I fiddled with the heart pendant around my neck, a symbol of better days, and wondered where the magic had gone.

In my mind, Malia was the wedge driving us apart. Despite Zack's protests that they were just friends, doubt gnawed at me. Was I losing him to her?

Sleep was elusive. All I could think was—Worst. Anniversary. Ever.

⋆ ⋆ ⋆ ⋆ ⋆

"I THINK Zack's gonna dump me," I blurted out, the words tumbling out before I could reel them back in.

The soft morning light trickled through my curtains, trying to paint the room in a comforting glow, but it was a lost cause. Clutching my phone, I lay curled up in my bed, a tangle of sheets and turbulent thoughts. I'd watched the clock all night, and as soon as it seemed a semi-decent hour, I called Emma.

On the other end of the line, Emma sounded like she was swimming up from the depths of sleep. "V? What time is it?"

"It's seven," I whispered, feeling guilty for dragging her into my drama so early.

"Why're you calling me on a Saturday at this ungodly hour?" She yawned, a sound that painted a vivid picture of her groggily fighting off sleep.

"Did you even hear what I said?" I could feel my voice cracking.

"Yeah, I heard you." There was rustling on her end, probably Emma sitting up in bed. "Why do you think Zack's going to break up with you?"

The memory of last night was like a bitter pill. "He took me to some action movie for our anniversary, barely said two words the whole night, then dropped me home with some lame excuse about an early shift today."

"Oh," was all she managed.

"That's all you can say? Oh?" I couldn't hide my frustration.

"Hold on a sec, I'm barely awake here." Her voice was muffled, likely from burying her face in a pillow.

"What am I going to do, Em?" My voice was desperate, searching.

"I honestly don't know, V. I'm so sorry," she said, her tone now more alert and concerned.

Feeling a sudden urge to cry, I quickly said, "Okay, I'll let you go back to sleep. Bye."

"No, V, hold on—" But I'd already hung up. Admitting my fears out loud made them too real, too tangible. And I couldn't ignore nature's call any longer.

Dragging myself out of bed, I shuffled to the bathroom, the events of the previous night replaying in my head like a bad movie. Every indifferent glance from Zack, every moment of silence, felt like a piece of the puzzle falling into place—a picture I didn't want to see but couldn't ignore.

Under the shower, I tried to rinse off the weight that was crushing my heart. The steam blurred the lines of reality, and for a moment, I allowed myself to drift in a world where Zack and I were still us. But the harsh reality always finds a way to creep back in.

Wrapped in a towel, I stood in front of the mirror, the fog slowly clearing. The girl who gazed back at me looked like a stranger—puffy-eyed, a shadow of her usual self. I wondered when the cracks in our relationship had started to spider-web out. Was it Amanda's sudden death? Malia's return? My mom's illness? Zack and I had both been hit hard, but instead of leaning on each other, he'd retreated into a shell I couldn't crack.

Downstairs, the house was still asleep. I made coffee, the ritual offering a small comfort, the warmth of the mug soothing against my palms. Sitting at the kitchen table, I stared out the window, watching the morning light play on the lawn. My phone lay next to me, silent and accusing—reminding me of the conversation I dreaded but needed to have. Part of me wanted to call Zack, to demand answers, but another part feared what those answers might be.

I knew I couldn't hide in my room forever, couldn't ignore the inevitable. But for now, in the quiet of the morning, I let myself pretend that everything was still okay. Just for a little while longer.

THE REST of the day was filled with mundane activities. I went to Scotty's soccer game just to get out of the house and give myself something to do, a distraction from my turbulent heart.

But as I sat there, surrounded by the enthusiastic shouts and cheers around me, my longing for Zack's presence only deepened.

I compulsively checked my phone, each glance filled with hope and then disappointment. No word from Zack. Zip. Nada. Nothing. No apologetic text or check-in. His silence was like a void, amplifying my fears.

The game ended in a victory for Scotty's team, with Scotty kicking in the winning goal. Dad, ever the proud coach, herded the team off for a celebratory pizza. Since I had no appetite for celebrating, I headed home.

Dinner was a quiet affair with Mom. The clink of our forks against the plates was like an awkward conversation. When she finally asked what was wrong, the dam broke. I recounted the devastating details of last night's anniversary.

She listened quietly until my words tapered off. Then she wrapped her arms around me, a comforting embrace like a warm blanket and held me while I cried. What did it say about us that Zack could be so absent, so disconnected, on a day that should have meant something to both of us?

I realized that the doubt and disappointment I felt were about more than just a ruined anniversary. In that quiet kitchen, with the empathy of a mother's hug, I confronted the painful truth that I deserved more.

BY NOON SUNDAY, when I still hadn't heard from Zack, a restless energy took hold of me. I threw on my comfiest hoodie and grabbed Lucky's leash, craving the fresh air and rhythmic motion of a walk to clear my head. Lucky, my enthusiastic companion, matched my brisk pace, his tail wagging in a blur as we navigated the familiar streets of our neighborhood.

I was so lost in my own head that I almost didn't notice Brian, one of Zack's co-workers from Skaterz, until he called out my name from across the street.

"Hey, V! Sup?" Brian said, jogging over, a big smile on his face.

"Hi, Brian. I'm okay," I lied, forcing a smile.

Brian's expression shifted, a flicker of hesitation in his eyes before he spoke. "Saw Zack out last night. Looked like he was having a blast."

His words were like a gust of cold wind, leaving me momentarily breathless. Zack had been out having fun? Without me? While I was at home, agonizing over our relationship, he was out enjoying himself as if nothing was wrong.

"Oh, really? Where?"

"At Kevin's party. He was really into it," Brian replied, unaware of the impact of his words.

"Thanks, Brian," I managed to say, my voice steady but my heart racing.

As he waved bye and strolled away, I felt like I'd just been sucker-punched.

The remainder of the walk was lost to me, my surroundings a backdrop to the turmoil inside. Lucky's occasional tug on the leash was the only thing anchoring me to the present.

Once home again, I retreated to the sanctuary of my room, lying on my bed, staring blankly at the ceiling. The ceiling stared back at me, a blank canvas for my thoughts. The walls felt like they were closing in, mirroring the tightness in my chest. The chasm between Zack's carefree night and my own anguish was painful. Were we drifting apart? We seemed to be on different pages, or maybe even in completely different stories.

Dinner was a quiet event, my parents casting worried glances my way. Their silence was a tacit acknowledgment of the storm brewing inside me. As the evening shadows grew longer, so did my reflections. It wasn't just about Zack anymore; it was about me, my value, my needs. What did I really want in a partner? Was I settling for less than I was worth?

I decided that tomorrow would be the day of reckoning with Zack. A showdown threatened, a pivotal moment that would either reset our course or mark the end of the road. It felt like standing at a crossroads, with each path leading to an unknown future. One future filled with possibilities, the other with the kind of heartache that's necessary for growth. But either way, it was a confrontation that couldn't be avoided any longer.

34

THE TURNING TIDE

The January sun cast a warm glow over the beach as Zack's car pulled into the parking lot. We'd ignored each other all day. But, as I exited the art room at the end of the day, I saw Zack waiting outside and looking uneasy.

"Hey, V," he said, his voice lacking its usual warmth. "Can we talk? Maybe go for a drive?"

I nodded, hands suddenly clammy. This was it—the moment of truth.

Palm trees swayed gently in the breeze, their shadows dancing on the sand, oblivious to the tension that hung between us. People milled around, laughter and chatter filling the air, a normal day for them, an increasingly confusing one for me.

"Why here, Zack?" I asked as we walked toward the water, the sound of the waves a rhythmic backdrop to my racing thoughts.

"I just . . . we need to talk. And I wanted to be somewhere you'd hear me out," he said, his voice strained.

We found a secluded spot, away from the prying eyes and

ears of beachgoers. The ocean stretched out before us, vast and unending, mirroring the chasm I felt opening up inside.

Zack took a deep breath, his usual easygoing demeanor replaced by an uncharacteristic seriousness. "Violet, I care about you a lot, but I can't keep pretending that everything's okay. My feelings . . . they've changed."

His words hit me like a rogue wave, unexpected and over-whelming. "Changed how? Zack, what are you saying?"

He wouldn't meet my eyes, his gaze fixed on a point beyond the shoreline. "I'm saying that I can't be with you anymore. I'm sorry, V. There's someone else."

The world seemed to pause for a moment, the sounds of the beach fading into a distant hum. "Malia?" The name came out as a whisper, a last piece of a puzzle I didn't want to complete.

Zack nodded, finally looking at me with a mix of regret and resolve. "Yes. It just . . . happened."

I felt a numbness spreading through me, a defense against the sharp sting of betrayal. I wanted to scream, to cry, to ask a million questions, but instead, I found myself standing up, steadied by a sudden clarity.

"I see. Well, thanks for not leading me on any longer," I said, my voice surprisingly steady. "How long have you felt this way about her?"

Zack sighed, the weight of the world seemingly on his shoulders. "I don't know. It's always been there, I guess. But when she came back, it was like a wake-up call. I can't deny it anymore. I'm sorry, V. You deserve someone who's all in." He turned to begin walking back, his steps heavy with resignation.

But I wasn't about to let him off the hook that easily. The detective in me needed answers. "Truth or dare?" I called out.

He stopped in his tracks. "What?" he asked, not bothering to turn around.

"You heard me. Truth or dare?"

"Come on, V. Not now."

I stepped in front of him, arms crossed, blocking his path. I glared at him. "Truth. Or. Dare."

He sighed like a deflating balloon. "Fine. Truth."

"Where'd you get the nickname 'Crash'?"

He looked incredulous. "Seriously? Now?"

"Yes, now."

"Why does it matter?"

I held his gaze, unflinching.

"It's a skater thing—we all have nicknames. You wouldn't get it."

"Enlighten me."

"It's just a dumb nickname. Can we please not do this?"

"But why 'Crash'? And why did you keep it after you moved here?"

He shifted uncomfortably. "Some of the skaters at school knew me by that name. They brought it back."

"And?"

"And what?"

"Answer the question. How did you get it, Zack? 'Crash'?"

Zack ran a hand through his hair, his frustration mounting. "Okay, so a few years back, I was at this skate park back in my old 'hood. Nailed this trick I'd been working on forever. It was pretty chill. Everyone was hyped, high-fiving, the works. Then this dude barrels into me. I took a nasty fall, got all scraped up. He felt bad, started calling me Crash, 'cause, you know, he crashed into me—"

"You're lying," I interjected sharply.

He looked taken aback. "No, I'm not. Well, I mean, that did happen, but it's not the real story behind Crash. How'd you know?"

"You have a tell," I said, keeping my voice steady.

He looked puzzled. "A what?"

"When you lie or dodge the full story, your hands get sweaty and you wipe them on your jeans."

He glanced down at his hands as if they'd betrayed him. "Oh." He let out a resigned sigh. "Alright, truth is, I got dared to do something really stupid, and I went for it." He stopped there, as if weighing whether to continue.

"What did you do, Zack?" I pressed, my voice steady despite the storm brewing inside me.

He nearly whispered, "I kissed Malia," refusing to meet my eyes.

I sucked in a breath and then held it, my stomach churning. The suspicion I'd harbored was now confirmed.

He didn't notice my reaction so he continued, "Like I said, it was stupid. Some jerk told her about the dare. She was furious. Punched me right in front of everyone. Someone yelled, 'Look, it's a Mack attack!' And another dude added, 'Ooh, crash and burn!' Then a third guy said, 'Dude, you crashed hard!' They were all laughing and pointing at me. Before I knew it, they were all chanting, 'Crash! Crash! Crash!' It stuck."

"I see. So, Malia was just a friend?" I asked, my voice laced with skepticism.

"Yes. It was dumb. We were kids. It didn't mean anything. Was a mistake."

"And our first kiss? You told me that was your first kiss *ever*. Was that a mistake too?"

"No! That dare when I was 13? It doesn't count."

"Right. Convenient. So, since you and Malia were always 'just friends,' but now you're with her, then that must mean our whole relationship doesn't count either, right? Because you've been secretly pining for her, and I'm the one who means nothing."

"No, you're twisting my words!"

"Then tell me how it is, Zack. You haven't been in love with her all this time?"

"No! She was my best friend and we grew up together, but she was a tomboy, like one of the guys. I never saw her 'that way.' She was just a cool skater girl."

"And now?"

"It's . . . now . . . she's different."

I felt hot tears stinging my eyes. "No kidding."

"Days after the dare, her family had to move back to Hawaii. It was sudden. We didn't get to say goodbye. I thought I'd never see her again. Now she's back, well, a lot happens between 13 and 16. Everything changed."

"Ya think? Thanks for finally telling me the truth, *Crash*. Now I know where I stand." I turned and walked away, not sure where I was going but needing to be away from him.

He called after me, but I couldn't stop. It was over.

When I got back to the parking lot, Emma was waiting by her mom's car, a worried look on her face. Zack had texted her, a detail I'd missed in the confusion of the moment. A silent understanding passed between us; she was here to take me home.

"Ready to go?" she asked softly.

I nodded, grateful for her presence. As we drove away, leaving Zack behind, the weight of the whole ordeal began to sink in. I was free of the lies and doubts, but at what cost?

THE HUM of the car engine filled the silence as Emma drove me away from the beach, away from Zack and the shattered pieces of what I thought was a perfect relationship. I stared out the window, watching as palm trees and storefronts blurred together in a dizzying array of colors and shapes. Emma glanced over at me occasionally, but neither of us spoke. What was there to say?

The numbness that had enveloped me at the beach began to wear off, replaced by a dull ache that throbbed with every beat of my heart. I replayed Zack's words in my mind, each syllable a tiny dagger. "There's someone else." The phrase echoed, growing louder and more insistent. Malia. The image of her laughing at their inside jokes, touching his arm, working late all those nights together . . . it was too much.

I squeezed my eyes shut, trying to block out the memories, but they came unbidden. Zack and I walking hand in hand, planning our future, making promises that now felt as flimsy as the paper napkins we'd doodled our dreams on.

At last, the floodgates opened and I told Emma the whole story, even the end when I had challenged Zack to 'Truth or Dare.'

"What would you have said if he'd picked dare instead of truth?" Emma asked.

"Easy. I would have said, 'I *dare* you to tell me how you got your nickname.'"

Emma laughed, her lilting tone was sweet music to my ears. "Oh, sorry," she apologized.

"Don't apologize. I love your laugh," I said. "Besides, I take myself way too seriously."

Emma stopped at a red light, and I caught my reflection in the side mirror. My eyes looked dull and lifeless. I was a wreck.

As Emma resumed driving, I realized the pain I felt was

more than just the loss of Zack. It was the crumbling of a belief I'd held onto so tightly. I thought love was simple, that it was enough. But maybe love was more complex and unpredictable than I had imagined.

"Thanks for being here, Em," I said, turning to look at her.

She smiled, a small, sad smile. "Always, V. You know I've got your back."

As we pulled up to my house, I hesitated before getting out of the car.

Sensing my hesitation, Emma said, "I know this is rough. But you're one of the strongest people I know. You'll get through this."

I managed a weak smile, wiping the last of my tears. "Thanks, again. I just feel so . . . blindsided. And stupid."

"You're not stupid. Zack's the stupid one. He lost someone amazing."

"Yeah, I am pretty amazing, aren't I?" I winked.

"The most amazingly stubborn, and not at all conceited—"

"Hey, that doesn't sound like a compliment anymore." I laughed. "But, I just thought Zack was different." I stared at my hands. "I thought we had something real. And now, I'm just the girl who got dumped for someone else."

Emma reached over, squeezing my hand. "You are so much more than that. You're smart, talented, and you have a big heart. Zack's decision doesn't define you."

We hugged, I thanked her again, and got out of the car, my feet carrying me automatically to the front door.

As I walked inside, the house welcomed me with its familiar embrace. My parents, seeing my tear-streaked face, wrapped me up in their hugs, offering wordless support. In that moment, surrounded by their unconditional love, I knew I'd be okay. Life would go on, and so would I, stronger and wiser for having faced my first painful heartache.

"What if I never find someone who really loves me for me?" I asked Mom.

"Sweetie, you're sixteen. You have your whole life ahead of you to find love. And when you do, it will be with someone who truly appreciates and understands you," Mom said, her eyes full of empathy.

As I SHUT the door behind me, I leaned against it, letting out a breath I didn't even realize I'd been holding. My room, a patchwork of movie posters and snapshots of better days, wrapped around me like a familiar embrace. I moved to the edge of my bed, shoes hitting the floor with a soft thud.

Finally alone, the mask fell away. Tears broke free, hot and unyielding, carving tracks down my cheeks. My sobs were the sound of heartbreak, for the love lost, for the dreams that turned to dust, and for the girl who once believed love was as eternal as the stars.

My gaze wandered to the collage of photos on my wall, zeroing in on a pic of Zack and me at the beach; our favorite spot. Our smiles, once symbols of a carefree love, now felt like relics of a bygone era. I took the photo down, placing it face down on my desk. It was a small act, but it felt like a step toward healing.

Next, I pulled out my journal and flipped it open to a blank page. The pen hovered for a moment before the words started spilling out. The hurt, confusion, and anger. But as I kept writing, the words flowed more freely, a release of all the emotions I'd bottled up inside.

I wrote about Zack, about us, about the sting of feeling replaced and forgotten. But I also wrote about my own dreams. I was more than just Zack's girlfriend. I had my own story to write.

I closed the journal, a newfound clarity beginning to emerge from the chaos of my emotions. Yes, I was hurt, and true, healing wouldn't happen overnight. But I was also strong, driven, and full of unexplored potential. The tears dried up, replaced by a quiet determination. I had a mystery to solve and a life to reclaim. I would rebuild, piece by piece, beginning with the girl in the mirror.

35

THE LONGEST DAY

News of my breakup with Zack had spread like wildfire through the school, turning me into the latest piece of juicy gossip. I felt eyes on me, whispers trailing in my wake, as I navigated the hallways with a stoic façade.

In APUSH, I arrived early, deliberately choosing a seat in the front row. I couldn't bear the thought of sitting near Zack, of feeling his presence so close yet so far removed. The space between us, once filled with shared glances and whispered jokes, now felt like a chasm.

Third period was a small respite, with AP Lit offering the comfort of Emma's familiar presence. She slid into the seat beside me, her eyes brimming with concern. "Hey, you holding up okay?" she whispered, her voice a soft anchor in a sea of turmoil.

I managed a nod, my smile more a grimace. "Yeah, just tired, you know?" It was the truth, but not the whole truth.

She patted my shoulder, a silent vow of solidarity. "I'm here for you, V. Always." Her words were comforting, yet they couldn't seep deep enough to soothe the hollow ache in my heart.

But fourth period loomed like an imminent storm—Psychology with Malia. The thought of sitting in the same room with her, pretending to be engrossed in the lecture while my world crumbled, was almost too much. I contemplated skipping, weighing the consequences against the turmoil brewing inside me.

Finally deciding against it, I walked into the class resigned to whatever awaited. Malia was already there, her eyes briefly meeting mine before looking away. Many unspoken words passed between us in that brief instant. The tension was thick, an invisible barrier erected where none had been before. I guess now that she had my boyfriend, there wasn't a reason to be nice to me anymore. All pretenses of her act were gone.

Lunchtime was a battlefield of emotions. Our usual table, once a haven of laughter and shared secrets with Emma and Zack, was occupied by others, its legacy seemingly erased overnight. I retreated to a secluded spot at the far end of the quad, my appetite a casualty of my heartache.

Emma found me there but apologized that she'd just been called to her coach's office. "See you in Art," she said, giving my shoulder a squeeze before disappearing.

I listlessly picked at my food, my mind wandering to Jacob's cheating ways. It was a welcome escape. I pulled out my notebook, immersing myself in possibilities and leads to follow up on. Each observation, each note was a step away from my personal anguish, a dive into a problem I could solve.

The rest of the day dragged on, my last two classes, AP Physics and Art, forgettable. The voices around me faded into background noise. The final bell was a relief, the sanctuary of my room at home calling me.

As I walked out of the school gates, the weight of the day settled on my shoulders. The world continued to spin, indifferent to the fact that for me, everything had changed. Tomorrow was another day, another stretch of hours to endure. But for now, the longest day had come to a close.

ONCE HOME, I ran upstairs to my room. After the day I'd just had, I needed some time to myself. Finally, with the door clicked shut, the dam of my emotions broke. Tears cascaded down my cheeks in a silent release. I cried for my lost love, for Zack, for the harsh realities of life I was beginning to understand.

A soft knock at my door pulled me from my reverie. "V? May I come in?" It was Mom, her voice gentle.

I wiped my tears away, sat up, and said, "Yeah, Mom."

She entered, her steps hesitant, and sat on the edge of my bed. "You've always wanted me to share news, good or bad, right?" Her eyes met mine, holding a gravity that commanded my full attention.

I nodded, swallowing the lump. "Yes, of course, Mom."

She took a deep breath, her hands clasped tightly in her lap. "But it's one of those things . . . you have to really want to know. Because once you know . . ."

"You can't un-know," I finished for her, dread setting in. "I want the truth, Mom. Always. Honesty fosters trust."

Her gaze faltered slightly. "You don't trust me?"

"It's not that. It's just that you haven't always been upfront with me."

"I was trying to protect you," she whispered.

"I know. But, whatever this is, I'm going to find out eventually. Wouldn't you rather have me by your side, through both good and bad?"

She smiled, a trace of sadness in her eyes. "How did I raise such a wise young woman?"

"Don't get all mushy on me. What's the news?"

Her expression turned serious. "They found a 3.5 cm mass on my skull bone, right here," she pointed to a spot above her left ear. "They don't think the cancer has spread to the brain, but I need targeted radiation. Chemo can't penetrate the skull."

My heart plummeted. "Anything else?"

"Dr. Khatri said the cancer returned faster than usual, probably due to the break in treatment with those infections."

"When's your radiation treatment?"

"Tomorrow."

I stood, resolute. "I'm going with you."

"V, sweetheart, I appreciate it, but I'll be in good hands. Dad and Grandma are coming. You have school."

I shook my head, determined. "I can miss a day. I need to be there. I'm going."

Her eyes met mine with gratitude and concern. "Alright," she conceded.

36

INKED WITH LOVE

The ride to Mom's radiation appointment was filled with Grandma's nonstop chatter, a welcome distraction from the anxiety gnawing at me. I half-listened, my fingers busily texting Emma to explain my absence from school.

Walking through the hospital halls, the hum of medical equipment from nearby rooms felt eerily familiar, reminiscent of those days visiting Amanda at this same hospital. I pushed the memories aside, smiling cheerily for Mom. Dad and Grandma were doing their over-the-top cheer routine, and Mom, bless her, seemed to soak it in. My mom, ever the fighter against this relentless enemy, displayed a quiet courage that was nothing short of heroic.

After the appointment, we returned home, each of us exhaling a collective sigh of relief. Mom's strength was awe-inspiring, but the physical signs of her battle were painfully visible. A bald patch now adorned her head.

I had prepared a little surprise for her the night before. "I have just the thing for that," I announced, a mischievous glint in my eye. "Stay there. I'll be right back."

I raced upstairs, brimming with excitement. Rummaging through my drawer, I found the temporary tattoo I had picked up—a bold red heart with 'MOM' stylishly scripted across it. It was perfect, a small gesture to bring a smile to her face.

"Check this out," I announced, holding the tattoo up triumphantly. "May I?" I asked, my eyes dancing with hope.

Her eyes lit up, a sparkle of her old self shining through. "Oh, V, that's adorable!" she laughed, giving her approval. Her giggle was infectious, and soon we were all giggling, a moment of lightness amid the gravity of our situation.

Carefully, I applied the tattoo to her bald spot, transforming it into a symbol of love. "There, now that's a fashion statement," I joked.

Grandma, who had been quietly observing, declared, "That's a lovely tattoo, dear. You should get a permanent one!" Her words brought another round of laughter.

Mom's reflection in the mirror was more than just a woman with a tattooed bald patch; it was a portrait of courage, adorned with the love of her family. For a brief moment, the weight of our journey seemed lighter.

As the day wore on, that small tattoo became more than just ink on skin—it was a badge of honor, a testament to the love and strength that held our family together. In that tiny, heartfelt gesture, we found a semblance of normalcy, a reminder that even in the darkest times, there were moments of joy to be found.

THE NEXT FEW DAYS, a familiar storm hovered over our home, as Mom braved a new round of chemo. She donned her battle armor—a T-shirt proclaiming, "REDHEADS ARE SUNSHINE MIXED WITH A LITTLE HURRICANE"—embodying her fighting spirit once again.

This time, gearing up for "Chemo Round 3," we brought back our head-shaving ritual, a symbol of our united front. Unlike the pixie cut from two years ago, Mom now placed her trust in Scotty and me to take charge with the electric clippers, under Dad's watchful eye, obviously. Following her instructions, we carefully left a uniform quarter-inch of hair, feeling like pros. Through the buzz of the clippers, Mom's smile was like this powerful light, showing us what real bravery looked like. And when her friend Rebecca dropped by with a brand-new wig for Mom, it was like a tiny win in this ongoing battle.

But the storm intensified. Post-chemo, clumps of stubble began to desert her, like leaves abandoning their branches in the first chill of autumn, scattering across her face, shoulders, and clothes. In a moment of bizarre humor, Dad transformed a dust buster into an impromptu barber tool, vacuuming Mom's head as we all laughed through our worries. It was absurd, yet strangely uplifting.

During these tempestuous days, I found solace in eavesdropping on Mom's phone conversations, seeking scraps of hope. Once, I overheard her say, "Day four after chemo is the worst so far, but it just got a little better. Dogs are amazing! Especially our Lucky. I just love our sweet dog." Peering into her room, I saw Lucky curled at her feet, a silent guardian against the gloom.

Weeks later, the clouds began to part. Mom's voice, filled with triumph, broke the news: "The chemo combo is working! My tumor markers dropped by 150—take that, you mutated cells!" She likened her journey to a marathon, acknowledging the rough patches but looking forward to a euphoric 'runner's high' post-recovery.

Toward the end of her call, I overheard her talking about Scotty and me. "Violet and Scotty are staying strong and helping out so much. I get hugs and kisses the moment they get home from school," she said.

This daily ritual of greeting my mom had become more than just a simple act; it was a source of comfort for both of us. It reassured me that, in my own small way, I was making a difference. Knowing that my hugs brought her even a moment of relief gave me the strength I needed to journey through this storm alongside her, every step of the way.

37

SEEKING TRUTH AND JUSTICE

T he quad buzzed with the usual lunchtime chatter, a vague and distant white noise I blocked out, firmly entrenched in my newly reinvigorated mission to catch Jacob at whatever it was he and his friends were caught up in. Hunched over my notebook, I jumped when a dark shadow appeared over me.

He sat at my table, breaking the invisible barrier I had built since he dumped me a week earlier. "Can we talk?" he asked, his voice hesitant.

I closed my notebook, feeling a knot tighten in my stomach. "What is there to talk about, Zack?"

He fidgeted with the phone in his hand, clearly out of his comfort zone. "I just . . . I wanted to make sure you're okay."

"I'm fine," I replied, my voice icy. The last week had been a carousel of emotions, and his presence wasn't helping. "You made your choice, Zack. Now, I'm making mine."

He nodded, a look of defeat on his face. There was a pause, a moment where I saw the old Zack, the one who cared. "I heard about your mom. How's she doing?"

I raised an eyebrow, skeptical. "Do you really care?"

"Yes, V! Of course I care. I adore Mrs. J."

A part of me softened, but I was careful not to let it show. "Her doctors say the chemo is working and the cancer is shrinking. It seems like good news, but the chemo is making her weak and she's in a lot of pain. She'll feel stronger again when this round of chemo is over."

"Good. I'm glad it's working. Bummer about the awful side effects though. Take care."

I watched him walk away, my heart a tangle of hurt and confusion. There was a time when Zack walking away would have left me shattered, but now, it was different. Yes, the pang of hurt still lingered, but it was overshadowed by my growing resolve. I had more important things to focus on, like my mom's battle, my own healing, and this case. The notebook in front of me beckoned—I had to solve this thing.

DRAGGING my feet to my last class, I felt the weight of the day. Zack's unexpected lunchtime appearance stirred up a storm of emotions I didn't want to deal with. I just wanted the day to end.

When Emma walked into the Art room, her usual brightness seemed out of place, annoying me somehow. Needing an outlet for my frustration, I pounced. "Where were you at lunch today?"

She blinked, taken aback. "I had an appointment with my counselor. Why?"

"Why didn't you mention it third period?" I pressed on, my tone edgy.

"I forgot," she answered, her confusion growing. "What's your problem?"

"You left me alone at lunch today."

Emma sighed, a note of weariness creeping into her voice. "I'm sorry, V, I know you're going through a lot, but I have needs too."

Her response was like a splash of cold water. Guilt twisted in my gut. "I'm sorry I snapped at you. But Zack visited me at lunch today."

Her eyebrows shot up. "Oh? What did he want?"

"He said he was just checking in to see if I was okay, and that he'd heard about my mom."

"Oh, that seems nice. Is that bad?" Emma asked, confused.

I scoffed. "It just makes it harder to forget him. I need him to leave me alone so I can forget about him."

"But, is there a slight possibility that you two could remain friends?" Emma asked gently.

I shot her a look, my emotions raw.

"Too soon?" she winced.

"Definitely. Too soon."

Mr. Slauson glanced our way, a gentle reminder in his tone. "Ladies, more drawing and less chatter, please."

"Sorry," we both muttered, turning back to our art assignments.

I picked up my charcoal, the rough texture grounding me. For me, art was more than just a class; it was a refuge. Here, amid the smell of paint and the quiet scratching of pencils on paper, I could momentarily put aside the chaos of heartbreak and worry, losing myself in the lines and shades of my drawings.

THE SCHOOL LIBRARY WAS QUIET, a few scattered whispers. I opted to stay at school instead of my usual going-directly-home-to-check-on-Mom routine. I needed a change in scenery. I immersed myself in a sea of notes and scattered evidence, breathing in the comforting, musty aroma of old books.

As I pieced together the connections between the pages, a fire kindled within me. This quest was transforming into something deeply personal. It was about proving to myself that I was more than just a girl who got dumped by Zack. I felt my identity shifting. I was a seeker of truth and justice, a solver of intricate puzzles, a mind capable of untangling webs of complexity.

The intensity of my focus made the world around me fade away. The occasional rustle of pages and distant footsteps of fellow students were mere background noise to the symphony of my thoughts. I was so engrossed in my work that time became a secondary character in the narrative of my concentration.

It wasn't until the librarian's gentle voice broke through my reverie that I realized how late it had gotten. "We're closing up, V," Miss Paroo said, with a kind but firm tone.

Startled, I looked up, blinking as if waking from a dream. The clock on the wall confirmed that hours had slipped by in what felt like moments. I hastily gathered my papers and notes —pieces of a puzzle I was still determined to put together— and packed them into my backpack.

Stepping out into the evening air, I felt somehow renewed. The sky was a canvas of twilight blues and purples, the first stars beginning to twinkle like distant beacons. As I walked, a chilly breeze seemed to whisper encouragements. My steps were no longer those of a girl burdened by heartache. They were purposeful, charged with a newfound determination.

This journey, this case I was unraveling, was a metaphor for my own life. Each clue, each piece of evidence was like a step toward understanding myself and the world around me. I was more than my circumstances, more than the pain of a breakup.

As the school building faded behind me, I felt a quiet confidence settling in. Tomorrow was another day, another opportunity to chase the truth, and another step toward becoming who I was meant to be.

38

CELEBRATING FAMILY

I woke up the morning of February 6th to a sky so clear and blue it seemed to mock the complexity of my life. Today was Dad's 43rd birthday, and despite all we were going through, I was determined to make his day special.

The scent of freshly brewed coffee wafted through the house as I made my way to the kitchen, where Mom was already in full party-planning mode. "V, can you grab the streamers from the closet?" she called out, her voice ringing with more strength than it had in weeks. Her ongoing battles and latest chemo round had left its mark on her, but today, she seemed to draw energy from the buzz of celebration in the air.

"Sure, Mom," I replied, happy to see her so full of energy, and glad she had the same idea as me—to make this day as special as we could for Dad.

I brought the box of party decorations into the kitchen and saw Dad, sitting on a stool at the counter, savoring his coffee in a rare moment of quiet bliss. "Happy birthday, Dad!" I greeted him cheerily, entering the kitchen.

"Thanks, V. Ready for another day?" His smile was wide and genuine. "Where's your brother?"

"Right here, Dad." Scotty danced into the kitchen with a piece of toast in his mouth, followed by Lucky who hoped to catch more than crumbs.

Mom took the box from me. "Thanks, V, I'll start decorating once you all head out." Still in her robe, she looked a little pale; yet I knew she was determined to make today special, no matter how she felt.

I hugged her before leaving for school. "Don't go overboard today," I whispered in her ear. "Remember to rest and leave some decorating for me."

She pushed me away and waved me off. "Go on, you'll be late. I'll be fine. Tonight is about celebration, and I want everything to be perfect for your dad."

We said our goodbyes and dispersed to our school day routines. I was excited about the party. It felt good to have something fun and festive to look forward to.

⋆ ⋆ ⋆ ⋆ ⋆

AFTER SCHOOL, Emma and I walked into a living room that had undergone a festive transformation. Streamers in vibrant colors crisscrossed the ceiling, balloons bobbed in every corner, and a large 'Happy Birthday' banner hung over the mantel. The atmosphere was electric and festive.

"Mmm, is that smell what I think it is?" Emma said, her nose perking up as she took in the delicious aromas wafting from the dining room.

The scent was unmistakable; a rich, enticing blend of spices and home cooking promised a culinary delight. As we moved closer, the dining table came into view, an array of dishes laid out like a tapestry of colors and textures—enough food to feed twenty people.

There was Arroz con Pollo, the rice and chicken perfectly seasoned, its aroma beckoning us closer. Beside it, a large bowl of Gallo Pinto, the beans and rice mixed in a dance of flavors, topped with a sprinkle of fresh cilantro. Platters of golden, flaky empanadas tempted my tastebuds, each one a little pocket of surprise, stuffed with savory fillings. A fresh ensalada rusa rounded out the feast with its creamy texture and coolness.

Emma and I exchanged glances, both wondering the same thing. "But Mom, how did you do all this?" I asked, turning to find her.

Looking more vibrant than she had in weeks, Mom wore a triumphant smile. "Easy. I had help. And you'll never guess who I picked up at the airport this morning."

Before we could even begin to guess, a familiar, cheery voice called out, "Surprise!"

We spun around to see Aunt Carmen, Dad's sister from Costa Rica, standing in the hallway with open arms and a beaming smile.

"Aunt Carmen!" I rushed to hug her.

"Look at you, little Violet!" Aunt Carmen exclaimed with joy. "You're blossoming into such a stunning young woman, just like the beautiful flower you are."

I felt the heat rush to my face, hoping she wouldn't pinch my cheek.

"Is this Emma, standing here? My, how you've transformed!" Aunt Carmen said with wide-eyed amazement. "You've grown into such a graceful and lovely young lady!"

"Hi, Carmen. Yeah, it's been quite a while. I think you last visited when I was about eleven," Emma replied with a smile.

"Ah, yes, that sounds about right. Are you still playing soccer?"

Just then, Scotty burst through the door. "Aunt Carmen!" He barreled into her, causing her to lose her breath.

"Scotty, be careful," I warned.

"Oh, that's nothing," Aunt Carmen said. "Growing up with five brothers, now that was something! So, where is the birthday boy? Where's my little Carlito?"

Dad walked in, stunned. "Sis?"

Aunt Carmen turned toward Dad with open arms. "Happy birthday, Carlito! Did you think I would miss this?"

Dad, still in disbelief, walked over and embraced her tightly. "Carmen, this is amazing! I can't believe you're here."

"Believe it, little brother," Aunt Carmen replied, patting his back. "I had to come and save the day in the kitchen, didn't I?"

Mom chuckled from the sidelines. "Hey, I'll have you know I was fully prepared to attempt a Tres Leches cake."

Aunt Carmen raised an eyebrow playfully. "Attempt being the operative word, eh?"

We all laughed, the room filling with a light, joyous energy. Aunt Carmen had a way of brightening every room she entered, her laughter infectious and her presence like a warm embrace.

Scotty, still hanging onto Aunt Carmen, grinned up at her. "Did you really make all the food, Aunt Carmen?"

"Of course, mijo," she winked at him. "Authentic Costa Rican dishes, straight from the heart."

Dad looked around at all the decorations and the spread on the table, a look of deep appreciation on his face. "You guys really outdid yourselves. This is perfect."

Emma nudged me gently, whispering, "Your family knows how to throw a party."

I nodded, taking it all in. "Yeah we do."

Just then, the doorbell rang, and a chorus of 'It's open!' echoed through the house. Friends and family began to pour in, each greeted by Aunt Carmen's exuberant hellos and Dad's grateful smiles.

As the room filled, Aunt Carmen nudged Dad playfully. "Now, Carlito, don't just stand there looking shocked all evening. Let's get this party started. I believe you owe me a dance."

Dad laughed, the sound mingling with the growing buzz of the party. "Only if you promise not to outshine me, Carmen."

"Oh, no promises there," she replied with a twinkle in her eye.

The evening was filled with laughter, conversation, and delicious food, all under the watchful eye of Aunt Carmen, the heart and soul of the celebration. It was more than a birthday party; it was a gathering of love, a celebration of family, and a reminder of our roots that stretched all the way to Costa Rica.

THE CLATTER of dishes and hum of conversations faded into the background as I found Dad standing alone on the back porch, gazing out into the night sky. The cool evening breeze carried the faint scent of jasmine, making the moment feel even more serene. I approached him quietly, holding the gift I had carefully chosen—a framed photo of the two of us on a recent hiking trip.

"Happy birthday, Dad," I said softly, handing him the gift. "I hope this year brings you immense joy and happiness."

He turned to face me, his expression softening as he took

the frame. The photo captured a moment of unguarded joy, both of us with wide smiles, surrounded by the beauty of nature. "Thank you, V. This means a lot," he said, his voice tinged with emotion. There was a depth in his eyes, a mix of gratitude and paternal love that only deepened our connection. "How are you holding up? I know things have been tough with Zack..."

I sighed. Looking at the stars, I found the words to express my turmoil. "I'm getting there. It's been hard, but I'm focusing on other things."

Dad nodded, a look of understanding in his eyes. He always had this uncanny ability to sense my struggles and offer wisdom without judgment. "Just remember, some things in life are out of our control. But how we respond to them, that's what defines us."

His words, simple yet profound, resonated with me. They were a gentle reminder of the strength I possessed, a strength he had always encouraged and nurtured in me. "Thanks, Dad. I'll remember that."

He put an arm around my shoulders, pulling me into a comforting side hug. "I'm proud of you, V. You're stronger than you realize, and no matter what happens, you always have your family to fall back on."

I leaned into his hug for a moment, a silent 'thank you,' then wanting to shift the focus, I asked, "How long is Aunt Carmen staying with us?"

"A couple of weeks, maybe longer. She's here to help out with your mom, take her to appointments, and, well, keep us from starving," he said with a playful wink. "And to give your grandma a well-deserved break. She's been our rock ever since, well, for as long as I can remember. She's finally taking some time to visit her sister in Portland, Oregon. Believe it or not, it was actually her idea to bring Carmen here."

I laughed. "Way to go, Grandma!" The thought of her finally taking some time for herself, amid everything she was doing for us, was reassuring.

Dad nodded, his eyes reflecting a mix of emotions. "Yeah, as mother-in-laws go, she's pretty amazing. It's good to have Aunt Carmen here, too. She brings a different energy, you know? And her cooking isn't too bad either," he added with a chuckle.

I smiled, looking around at our family and friends gathered in our home, the aroma of Aunt Carmen's cooking filling the air, the laughter and conversations. This moment, with all its simplicity and familial love, was a vivid reminder of the support system I had around me—a foundation of strength and love that could weather any storm.

We turned to head back inside, our brief exchange more than just a birthday wish or a fatherly pep talk. It was a reaffirmation of our bond, a reminder that no matter how complicated life got, the love between a father and his daughter remained a constant, unwavering force.

39
HEARTS AND DECEITS

aving Aunt Carmen in the house had been like a breath of fresh air. The kitchen was always brimming with the aromas of amazing foods being cooked, the house was impeccably clean, and she had become Mom's steadfast companion for all her hydration infusions and chemo appointments. I'd barely seen Mom all week, her time consumed by treatments and rest.

But this morning, Valentine's Day greeted me with an unexpected sight. On the kitchen table were heart-shaped pancakes, each with slices of plantain cooked into them. They seemed to mock me with a silent 'hi, loser.' I slumped into a chair across from Scotty, who enthusiastically devoured his breakfast.

"Happy Valentine's Day, V!" he mumbled through a mouthful of food.

"Ugh. Don't remind me. Today is going to suck. Where is everybody?" I reluctantly reached for a pancake and put it on my plate.

"Hospital. Mom has chemo. Dad says you have to take me to

school today," he replied, his focus more on the pancakes than our conversation.

"Oh, right. I forgot." I sighed, my appetite waning at the thought. "Hurry and brush your teeth then. We better get going."

At school, Valentine's Day was in full force. The cheerleaders were selling Heart-o-Grams, and the hallways looked like a Valentine's Day factory had exploded—pink and red glittered hearts were strewn everywhere.

In Pre-Calc with Mr. Sutton, my mind kept drifting back to memories of Zack. Our first date, first kiss, and even the times before we were 'official,' when I stubbornly called him by his skater name, Crash. Back when he adored me.

"V? I asked you a question," Mr. Sutton's voice snapped me back to reality.

"What? Oh, sorry, sir. Could you repeat the question?" I stammered, mentally kicking myself. Calc was the last place I should be zoning out, especially since I was barely maintaining a C+.

"Certainly. On last night's homework, what did you get for number 4?" he repeated, his tone patient but expectant.

I scrambled through my notes, feeling the eyes of the class on me. "Um, I got X equals 7.5," I answered, unsure.

The rest of the day was a blur of Valentine's excesses and my own inner turmoil. Emma couldn't understand my gloom. "It's just another day," she said as we walked to our lockers.

"You wouldn't understand. You've never had a boyfriend," I said, a bit too sharp.

"Ouch," she said, feigning indignation. "I'm not stupid, V. I know this is just basically a Hallmark holiday for couples. But I don't see why it matters so much. If you really love someone, you can make any day special. Why celebrate once a year with everyone else in some commercialized frenzy of store-bought flowers and chocolates?"

Her words made me pause. "That's a good point. You're right. Let's boycott this day!"

"Not quite what I was saying, but okay, I'm in. What'd you have in mind?" Emma asked, her spirits lifted by my sudden change of mood.

"How about an anti-romance movie marathon at my place?"

"Sure. But let's make it just one movie, okay? I've got a ton of homework."

"One it is, then."

As the day drew to a close, I reflected on Emma's words. Valentine's Day was supposed to be about love, and I realized that love came in many forms: the selfless love Aunt Carmen showed my family, the enduring friendship Emma and I had, and the love between a mother and a daughter ... that my mom demonstrated every day. Maybe I didn't have romantic love right now, but I wasn't devoid of love. And that was something to hold onto, especially on a day like today.

THE NEXT DAY AT LUNCH, Emma told me she had something to show me. "Remember when I told you I'd keep an eye on every-one's social media for clues?"

"Yes," I replied, my interest piqued.

"Well, I've seen a few intriguing posts, but then you sorta lost interest so I let it go. Anyway, this is the one that matters. I think this is big. Here, take a look." She pulled out her phone, swiping to an Instagram post. It was a meme of an anxious SAT taker, face flushed with stress. But the real hook was the engagement it received—over a thousand likes and a swarm of comments.

"Wait, it says here there's a 'test-taking whiz'?" I pointed out, squinting at the screen.

"Yeah, keep going. It gets better. Read the one from Jacob," she urged.

I scrolled down until Jacob's comment popped out. "Ace in the hole? Hole-in-one? How 'bout a known test-taking machine? U know what to do."

"Oh my gosh, Emma, this is huge!" I exclaimed, my voice trembling with excitement. "This could be the break we've been waiting for!"

"I know!" She mirrored my excitement. "But what does it mean? Jacob's not a test-taking machine." She scrunched her nose in disbelief.

"No, he's not," I agreed, feeling the pieces click into place. "But he knows someone who is."

"Meaning?"

"Meaning, there's a possibility that people are paying Jacob to arrange for this anonymous 'test-taker' to sit their exams for them."

"But how?" Emma's brow furrowed in confusion.

"That's what we need to figure out."

"Who could it be, though?"

"I might have a few ideas about that." A couple of names came to mind, students whose academic prowess was legendary, but they kept low profiles.

The lunch bell rang, cutting our conversation short. "We'll dig into this further after school," I promised as we gathered our things. "Thanks, Em! This is exactly what I need right now."

"Glad I could help."

AFTER SCHOOL, Emma came over and we plunged into an investigative frenzy, combing through social media for any hint of a connection between Jacob and academically gifted students at our school. The room was awash with the blue light from our screens as we sifted through post after post, comment after comment. We disregarded those who boasted about great SAT scores but had average grades. Those were false leads.

"But how would a 'test taker' take a test for someone else?" Emma pondered, her eyes still glued to her phone, finger paused mid-scroll.

"Easy. Make a fake ID," I suggested, leaning back in my chair and tapping my pen against my chin thoughtfully.

"How is that easy?" She looked up, her expression skeptical. The idea seemed far fetched, even in the light of our growing suspicions.

"Know any hackers?" I joked.

Emma's eyes widened, a spark of realization flickering in them. "Actually, I might."

The air between us crackled with the thrill of the chase. I leaned forward, eager to hear more. "Really? Who?"

"Our stat keeper, Miles Archer."

"Stat keeper?"

"Yeah, the Statistician for our team. He records and analyzes all the statistics from our games and practices. He's a senior and always bragging about bypassing school firewalls and stuff."

I nodded, feeling the gears in my mind turning. "Can you get in touch with him? See if he can make a fake ID? We need something that looks legit."

Emma hesitated, biting her lip. "That's kinda risky," she said. "Plus, I don't know him that well."

"I know, but we're onto something big here," I said, the urgency of our mission reigniting in my voice. "We can't let this slip through our fingers."

With a deep breath, Emma nodded. "Okay, I'll talk to Miles at our game tomorrow. But we have to be careful. If word gets out we're snooping around again, it could blow up in our faces."

"I know," I said. "But we've got to take that risk. It's the only way to find out who's behind this."

40
GOALS AND SCHEMES

Ensuring a front-row spot at Emma's soccer game was part of my latest plan. Admittedly, my attendance record at her games wasn't stellar, but today was about more than just supporting my best friend. It was about gathering intel, in true Emma and V style.

Perched on the bleachers right behind the team, I was in prime eavesdropping territory. Emma, usually a straight shooter, was about to approach the team's stat keeper, Miles. Word was he was quite the tech whiz.

"Hey Miles, got a sec?" Emma's voice was casual but purposeful.

Miles, looking like he'd just won the lottery, perked up. "Hey, Emma! Sure, what's up?"

I muttered to myself, "He's totally into her. This is perfect. We've got leverage."

I tried to catch Emma's eye, to give her a subtle nod of encouragement, but she ignored my attempts. She was in the zone.

I watched as Emma leaned in, doing this thing with her

ponytail I'd never seen before. "You're good with tech stuff, right?"

Miles straightened up, trying to look nonchalant. "Yeah, I guess I'm okay."

She bit her lip, giving him a look of admiration that I knew was all part of her act. "How hard is it to get a fake ID? Do you know anything about that?"

Miles shifted gears from flattered to intrigued. "A fake ID? It's doable for someone with the right skills."

Emma feigned innocence. "I really want to get into this bar next weekend. They've got this great band, but it's 21 and over."

Miles's reaction was comical, like he couldn't believe 'Emma the Soccer Star' wanted to hit a bar. "You want to get into a bar? That's cool."

I had to stifle a laugh. Emma, at a bar? More like Emma at a Harry Potter movie marathon.

"Could you help me out?" she asked, her voice the perfect blend of hopeful and flattering.

Miles was hooked. "I might know someone. I'll check."

Emma gave him her best 'you're my hero' smile and jogged back to the field.

I sat back, thoroughly impressed. Emma, the girl next door, pulling off a con like a pro? I couldn't help but feel pride. This just got a lot more interesting.

EMMA'S TEAM clinched the win, and I couldn't have been more proud. But it wasn't just her athletic prowess that had me buzzing. Our sleuthing breakthrough had my adrenaline pumping like I'd just downed a double espresso. I was so amped up, I could've kissed Emma right there. Who knew my bestie was such a dynamo both on and off the field?

Post-game, I wove through the crowd to congratulate her. "You killed it out there, superstar!" I cheered.

"Thanks! It's great you finally made it to one of my games," she replied, a hint of mischief in her eyes.

"It's not just your soccer skills I'm talking about," I said with a wink. "Your little dance with Miles was top-notch."

She rolled her eyes but couldn't hide the smirk. "Yeah, yeah, laugh it up."

"But seriously, you were a natural. I never pegged you for a 'covert ops' kind of girl."

She laughed, tucking a stray hair behind her ear. "Turns out, I can be quite the charmer when the situation calls for it. But let's not get ahead of ourselves. We still need to see if Miles delivers on that fake ID."

"True, but I've got a good feeling about this," I said, barely containing my excitement. "And hey, I'm not just proud of your game, but for stepping up big time today."

She softened. "Thanks, but you're the brain behind the operation. I'm just following your lead."

As we walked away from the field, I noticed some of Emma's teammates eyeing us curiously, probably wondering what mission impossible we were planning.

"So, what's our next move?" Emma asked.

"First, we wait for Miles. If he pulls through with the ID, we'll have to be super strategic about our next steps. How can we leverage this to flush out the real test-taker?"

Emma nodded, all business. "Got it. We play it cool and smart. One wrong move and we could blow our cover."

"Exactly. We need a foolproof plan. Maybe we set up a

meeting, pose as potential clients looking to hire the test-taker. Naturally, we'd need aliases."

Her eyes lit up with intrigue. "That could work. And Miles could be our ticket in."

Just then, Stephanie, one of Emma's teammates, bounded over, full of energy. "Emma! Team photo time!"

Emma's laughter rang out as Stephanie dragged her away. "Let's celebrate after you crack this case, detective," she called over her shoulder.

"Deal!" I shouted back, watching her disappear into the crowd, feeling admiration for my fearless, resourceful best friend.

41

THE FINAL STRETCH

Hunched over the kitchen table, I was half-heartedly scrolling through Instagram while my cereal turned soggy. The house had this hollow echo to it since Aunt Carmen left. I already missed her, especially her cooking. Just as I shoveled another spoonful of cereal, my scrolling came to an abrupt halt. A photo of Zack and Malia, all smiles, flashed on my screen. "Shoot!" I gasped, narrowly saving my cereal bowl from toppling over.

Scotty chomped on his Cap'n Crunch like it was his job. "V said a bad word!" he announced with the gusto of a courtroom judge.

"I did not. Pipe down, Scotty," I said, giving him a mock scowl.

Dad, leaning against the counter with his morning coffee, looked over. "What's wrong, V?"

I sighed, the weight of the day pressing down on me. "It's February twentieth."

Dad raised his eyebrows, prompting further explanation.

"It's Zack's birthday," I finally admitted, feeling the sting of those words.

"Oh," Dad and Scotty said in unison, exchanging a glance. Scotty couldn't resist a dramatic eye roll as he said, "Here comes the drama."

Dad tried to hide his smirk behind his coffee mug, but his eyes gave him away.

Frustrated and feeling the need to escape, I bolted upstairs to brush my teeth. But before I got in my car, I sent Zack a text.

It was an olive branch, if only a small one. Despite my confusion and hurt over his choice of Malia over me, part of my heart still stubbornly wished him well.

At school, Emma was waiting by my locker, her face a picture of understanding.

"Hey, V, you doing okay today?"

"I'm managing. Just another day, right?" I shrugged, putting on a brave face.

She gave me a knowing nod, her eyes reflecting the empathy I wasn't ready to face. "Just another day," she repeated, but we both knew it was anything but.

* * * * *

In APUSH, my heart did a strange little flip when Zack slid into the seat next to mine. "Hey, V," he said with a half-hearted wave.

"Hi, Zack," I replied, my voice cool and even, eyes fixed on my notebook.

"I, uh, wanted to thank you," he began, fumbling for words, "for the birthday text."

"No problem," I said, still not looking up. "We have history, Zack. I can't just erase that." I kept my tone steady, a mask over the whirlpool of emotions beneath. "And yes, I still care. Despite everything."

He nodded, visibly relieved. "I care about you too, V. Does this mean we can be . . . friends?"

"Maybe," I said, finally glancing up to meet his eyes. They were hopeful, yet cautious. "But no double dates or anything weird, okay?"

He let out a short, genuine laugh. "Agreed. Nothing weird."

There was a brief connection in his gaze, a hint of regret, maybe. But the tardy bell rang, severing the moment. Mr. Fox called for everyone's attention, and we both turned to face the front.

As I took notes during the lecture, my heart still hurt thinking about what we had and what could have been. But reaching out, being kind, felt better than carrying a grudge and cutting him out of my life completely. It was a small step, but it was a step forward, nonetheless.

Packing up at the end of class, I mulled over our conversation. Life's funny like that—throwing curveballs when you least expect them. One minute I was deep in relationship drama, the next I'm recalibrating my entire future.

With my rescheduled SAT date less than two weeks away, distractions were the last thing I needed. Emma's Prepped notes were like gold dust now, and I mentally reminded myself to snag them from her soon. A renewed sense of purpose coursed through me. It was time to buckle down and nail this test. Life might be full of surprises, but I was ready to tackle them head-on, one unpredictable, chaotic, lesson-filled day at a time.

I made my way through the crowded hallways, my mind shifting gears from past regrets to future plans. This test was a hurdle I didn't plan on jumping twice. Emma's notes, my focus, and a little bit of that Jiménez resilience were all I needed. Bring it on, SATs. I'm ready.

THE EVE of the SAT had finally crept up on me, a day that had been casting a long shadow in my mind for what felt like forever. There I was, camped out at my desk, surrounded by a fortress of prep materials: Emma's obsessively organized notes, my own jumble of scribbles, and the battered Prepped textbook that had seen better days. The room was quiet, the kind of hush that's thick with anticipation, broken only by the occasional rustle of a page or the faint scratch of my pen.

My desk lamp cast a warm glow in the dimness of my room, spotlighting my little world of study. Each note, each diagram was more than just academic work; they were markers on a personal journey that began way back in October. From the rollercoaster of my social life to the gut-punch of my mom's health scare, and not to mention the case I was determined to crack, it all seemed to funnel down to this moment.

Then came the buzz of my phone, slicing through the quiet. A message from Emma:

> Tomorrow's the big day! How are you
> holding up?

I glanced at the screen, feeling a swarm of butterflies in my stomach. This test was more than a bunch of questions; it was a finish line of sorts, the end of one crazy chapter and the jump into something new. I typed back, my fingers surprisingly sure:

> As ready as I'll ever be, I guess.

I set the phone aside and took a deep breath, letting the gravity of the moment sink in. There was an odd sense of calm amid the storm of nerves. The path to this SAT hadn't just been about hitting the books. It had been a journey of growth, of getting to know the real me.

This test wasn't just about the answers I'd circle tomorrow. It was a testament to my fortitude, to the lessons learned in the face of adversity, and to the strength I found in the support of friends like Emma. With a renewed sense of purpose, I turned back to my notes. They didn't seem like mere words and numbers anymore; they felt like old allies. This was the home stretch, and I was ready to take it head-on.

42

MOMENT OF TRUTH

I awoke Saturday morning with a mix of nerves and determination. The SATs were finally here, the endgame of months of grinding study sessions and a ticker tape of anxiety. The first rays of sunlight sneaked through my blinds as I sat up in bed, trying to shake the cobwebs of a restless night.

Surrounded by the battlefield of my room, where practice books and notes lay scattered, I took a moment to steady myself. Each breath was a conscious effort to tame the jittery butterflies staging a revolt in my stomach.

I opted for my battle armor—a soft blue hoodie and my lucky jeans, hoping they'd bring some semblance of comfort on this high-stakes day.

Mom sat across from me at breakfast, her worry lines deepening as she stirred her coffee absentmindedly. Our usual morning banter was replaced by a tense quiet, punctuated only by the clinking of cutlery and the occasional sip of coffee. We were both caught in the gravity of the day, swirling in our own seas of what-ifs and maybes.

"Good luck today, sweetie. You're ready for this," Mom broke the silence, her voice reassuring.

"Thanks, Mom. I just want to get it over with," I replied, offering a half-hearted smile, a façade to mask the internal chaos.

After a few more bites of my barely touched toast, I gathered my SAT survival kit: freshly sharpened pencils, a calculator humming with new batteries, and the golden ticket—my admission slip. Each item was a talisman, a reminder of the journey to this very day.

I slung my backpack over my shoulder, its weight a comforting, familiar presence. Stepping out into the bright morning, the world seemed oblivious to the storm inside me. The usual symphony of birds and distant traffic was a soothing contrast to the tumultuous thoughts in my head. I got in my car, rolled down my windows, and backed out of the driveway.

Today, I would face one of my biggest challenges yet. The weight of expectation, the months of preparation, and the uncertainty of the outcome all converged into this single day. It was more than just a test; it was a milestone, a rite of passage into what lay beyond high school.

I felt a resolve settling within me. I would face this challenge head-on, armed with my hard work and the support of those who believed in me. The drive to the testing center wasn't just a physical one; it was a drive toward a future that was mine to shape, one question at a time.

APPROACHING the test center at Orange High School, now morphed into a battleground of academic ambition for the

SATs, I felt the air crackle with a kind of nervous energy unique to these high-stakes tests. The front lawn was a mosaic of students, some pacing like caged animals, others sitting with crumpled notes clutched in their hands—all bound by the singular mission to slay the SAT dragon.

Among this sea of tense anticipation, I recognized Tessa from my SAT prep class. Her presence was a tiny island of familiarity in this ocean of anxiety. Like me, Tessa's face was etched with apprehension, her eyes darting around as if trying to gauge the competition.

"Ready to tackle this beast?" she asked, her attempt at cheer slightly strained as I joined her in the serpentine line leading into the building.

"Born ready," I lied, plastering on a façade of confidence. I shifted the weight of my backpack, armed to the teeth with pencils and calculators. "Didn't you take the test back in October?"

Tessa nodded, her expression turning a shade more serious. "Yeah, but it was a disaster. I've been hitting the books hard since then. This is my last chance, being a senior and all."

Her confession hit close to home. For many here, today was more than just another test; it was the final round in the ring. "Hey, knock 'em dead," I said, meaning it.

"Thanks, you too," she replied, her smile more genuine this time.

We fell into a subdued conversation, sharing our hopes and the strategies we'd picked up during the Prepped course. It was an attempt to ease the tension that clung to us, a thin veil over the undercurrent of stress and high stakes.

Around us, the atmosphere was a blend of ambition and anxiety. Some students were huddled in groups, going over last-minute tips, while others stood alone, earbuds in, lost in their last-minute prep. The air was filled with a mix of hushed voices and the rustling of papers.

Every now and then, the school's main doors would swing open, and a proctor would call out instructions, his voice cutting through the nervous chatter like a beacon guiding us to the imminent challenge.

As we shuffled forward, the reality of the moment really sank in. Beyond those doors lay the culmination of months of stress, hope, and ungodly amounts of caffeine. For some, like Tessa, it was the last roll of the dice for their college dreams.

Despite our attempts at casual conversation, the weight of the day was undeniable. Each shared story of preparation and tip exchanged, held the unspoken understanding that today was a day of reckoning.

The line inched closer to the entrance, and the flutter of nervous excitement in my stomach grew stronger. Today, each of us would face a challenge that was more than just about answering questions correctly; it was about proving to ourselves just how far our hard work and determination could take us. I was ready to face whatever this test threw at me. Bring it on.

THE MOMENT I entered the examination hall, a hush enveloped me, broken only by the occasional shuffling of papers and the distant, relentless ticking of a clock. The room was a checkerboard of desks, each a tiny island for a student locked in their own private battle with the SAT. Finding my designated spot, I inhaled deeply, opening my test booklet as the proctor signaled the start of the exam.

Laid out before me was the gauntlet, a complex labyrinth of text passages, complex equations, and a minefield of multiple-choice questions. Each page was a new challenge, a puzzle to be solved. I worked methodically, my pencil scratching against the paper, marking answers with precision. I tried to block out everything but the task in front of me, focusing solely on the words and numbers that danced before my eyes.

But even with months of prep under my belt, doubt slithered in, whispering toxic what-ifs and questioning my readiness. Each question felt like a skirmish, with my confidence and anxiety locked in a ceaseless tug-of-war.

Midway through a tricky math problem, a thought hit me like a cold splash of water. The SAT cheater case. The irony was almost laughable. Here I was, in the eye of the storm, sitting amid the very test that sat at the heart of my investigation. A test that for some, represented a sordid shortcut to success.

This epiphany yanked me back to reality. Suddenly, the clinical walls of the exam room seemed to fall away, revealing the larger narrative at play—the reason I'd been so invested in uncovering the truth. This wasn't just a battle of wits; it was a fight for justice. The SAT, in all its dreaded glory, was a symbol of fairness and integrity in a world where some chose the easy, dishonest path.

I refocused, fortified by the reminder of why this mattered. Every filled bubble was evidence of my dedication, a small victory for honesty over deceit. Amid the scribbling of pencils and ticking of the clock, I wasn't just a high school junior taking a test; I was a seeker of truth in a game where the stakes were far higher than just college admissions.

* * * * *

THE FIRST HALF of the test had left my mind swirling, a mix of algebraic formulas and passage analyses dancing through my thoughts. When break came, I was ready to clear my head. I welcomed the fresh air that greeted me outside.

Stretching, I caught sight of a familiar figure a few feet away. It was Lucas Bennett, our Prepped tutor, leaning against the school's stucco wall. He shouldn't be anywhere near here; he was supposed to be tutoring, probably lighting a fire under another batch of college hopefuls. Yet, here he was, decked out in a baseball cap that did little to disguise him.

Curiosity getting the better of me, I strolled over. "Lucas, what's the deal? Why are you here?" My voice was a mix of surprise and skepticism.

He glanced up, and for a split second, his mask slipped. There was a flash of something in his eyes—fear, maybe, or surprise. He stared at me, as if frozen in time. Then, as if someone hit fast-forward, he turned and bolted.

I watched, bemused and bewildered, as he vanished around the corner. "Well, that's one for the books," I muttered to myself, a half-laugh escaping my lips despite the bizarre situation.

This wasn't a random occurrence. Lucas Bennett, showing up at an SAT test center? It screamed 'suspicious.' And his reaction? That of a man with something to hide.

The break bell snapped me back to reality. I lingered a moment longer, piecing together this new development in my head. Lucas Bennett just became a key player in my investigation, and I had questions that needed answers.

As I stepped back into the testing room, my mind was split between the test and the mystery at hand. I needed to focus on the remaining sections, but a part of me was already plotting how to confront Lucas Bennett.

Settling back into my seat, I barely registered the proctor's voice. The test resumed, and while my pencil moved mechanically over the paper, my thoughts were racing ahead. I was eager for the test to end, to step out of the role of a student and get back on the case.

As I worked through the final questions, my determination solidified. Each answer I marked was a small defiance against whatever shady business Bennett was involved in. This test wasn't just about my future anymore; it was about standing up for what the SATs were meant to represent.

The final minutes ticked by, and I reviewed my answers, trying to keep my mind from wandering to Lucas Bennett. I closed my test booklet with a mix of relief and resolve. The SATs were over, but my mission was just ramping up. It was time to chase down an SAT test prep tutor.

As the proctor's final words echoed through the examination hall, a collective exhale swept through the room, echoing relief. We were like survivors of a shared ordeal, gathering our things in a daze of exhaustion and muted triumph. As I stepped out of the room, the tension seemed to dissipate into the air.

Outside, I saw Tessa again. Her face, though weary, was lit up with a sense of accomplishment. "We survived," she said, and we shared a laugh. The kind that's born from relief, tinged with disbelief and accomplishment.

"Yeah, we did," I agreed, feeling the weight of the past few months lifting, if only for a moment. Standing under the bright sun, I felt like we had done more than just survive a test. We overcame a significant hurdle.

We parted with simple goodbyes, each heading in opposite directions. As I walked away, I couldn't shake the feeling that this was more than just the end of an exam. It felt like the closing of a significant chapter in my life as well, both academically and personally.

Nearing my car, I kept a vigilant eye on the dispersing crowd. And then, as if fate had a sense of dramatic timing, I saw him—Lucas Bennett, in his not-so-incognito ball cap, sprinting toward the parking lot to my right. His attempt at a discreet escape was futile, almost comical.

I quickened my pace, my instincts kicking in, weaving between parked cars, closing the gap between us with determined strides. Then, stepping out from between two SUVs, I blocked his path. "Surprise," I said, a hint of triumph in my voice.

Lucas stopped abruptly, his eyes wide with surprise and guilt. "What do you want?" he demanded, his voice edged with defiance.

"You know exactly what I want," I replied, holding his gaze.

His posture faltered, and the floodgates opened. He was the man behind the curtain, taking the SATs for those willing to pay the price. His tone was a strange mix of bragging and confession as he proclaimed his ability to ace any test. But as he spoke, his demeanor shifted. "I never meant for it to go this far. I never should've gone along with it," he admitted, his voice dropping to a whisper, laden with a regret that seemed to weigh heavily on him.

"Wait? Aren't you the ringleader?" I prodded. "You're the test-taking wizard behind this whole thing, right? Jacob works for you. He recruits students who pay you to take the test for them. And you give him a cut."

"Not exactly. None of this was my idea, I swear. You have to believe me. I just got caught up in the easy money."

"If not you, then who's behind it?" I pressed.

He hesitated, then said, "I can't tell you."

"Why not? It's over, Lucas. You need to come clean," I urged.

He nodded, the fight draining from him, replaced by the long sigh of resignation. "I know. I'm going to turn myself in. And when I do, I'm going to make a deal with them before I start naming names. I'll deal with the authorities on my terms."

His words hung in the air, marking the end of one mystery and the beginning of another. He was a man trapped by his choices, now looking for a way out.

"You're turning yourself in," I echoed, respect mingling with surprise at his decision.

He nodded, his gaze finally meeting mine. "I have to," he said, his voice steadier now. "It's the only way to make things right. Not just for me, but for everyone involved."

I nodded, understanding the gravity of his choice. "I hope it brings you some peace," I said sincerely.

Lucas managed a wry grin. "Thanks."

With that, he turned and walked away, his steps resolute. I watched him go, feeling an unexpected sense of kinship. Our paths had crossed in the most unlikely of ways, yet in this shared moment of vulnerability, I felt a strange sort of gratitude.

As I got in my car, a victorious smile played on my lips. The pieces of the puzzle were finally falling into place, and I was one step closer to unraveling the entire scheme. If anything, this case had taught me to expect the unexpected and always be ready for what comes next.

43

ROAD TRIP

I flicked my phone to life to call Emma, my heart doing a dance in my chest. "Emma, brace yourself. I've got headline news!"

"Funny, I was about to say the same thing. Spill it."

"Patience, I'm on my way. And Em?"

"Yeah?"

"Keep your doors locked."

"We always do. Hurry!"

The drive to Emma's was a blur, my mind all about my news. When I pulled up, Emma was pacing outside, her eyes scanning the street like a hawk.

"We have a situation, a big break in the case," I blurted, barely out of my car.

"Tell me about it. Like, last years' entire senior class," she countered.

I raised an eyebrow quizzically. "Our Prepped tutor, Lucas Bennett, is playing a darker game than we thought."

She crossed her arms. "Suzie Denton, Stanford scholar, was one of the test-takers!"

We stared at each other, the puzzle pieces snapping together. "Hold up. Lucas and Suzie in the same sentence? Start from the top. And don't leave anything out—Suzie was my friend."

Emma furrowed her brows. "Lucas? Okay. One thing at a time, but you'll probably want to sit down for this. Stanford might need to reconsider their admissions. Come on, let's go inside."

When we got to Emma's room, we both flopped on her bed and she pulled out her phone. "You need to hear this. Wait, how'd your test go?"

"Really? Enough stalling. Whatever it is, I can take it. What ya got?"

"Okay . . . I overheard two seniors on my team talking in the locker room after our game today, which we won, by the way."

"Emma!"

"Right. Listen." She hit play.

The recording started with lockers slamming shut, then two distinct voices emerged:

"Hey, are you still trying for Valedictorian this year?"

"Of course. Besides, competition's not as fierce as last year. That Suzie Denton set a high curve."

"Yeah, but I heard at the last minute, they snatched the valedictorian title away from her. Something about cheating?"

"That was just rumors and hearsay; nothing was proven."

"But she made a killing with those SATs."

"Like I said, rumors."

"Are you sure? Jacob tried to get my sister to pay $2.5K for Suzie to take the test for her in October, guaranteeing her a score above 1560. And, the price went up to $3K per test just a month ago."

"Whoa. That's crazy."

"Totally."

The recording ended. Shaking my head, I quickly connected the dots. Suzie's perfect scores, Lucas's expertise, and Jacob's opportunism. It was a recipe for a deceitful enterprise, one that went far deeper than I had ever imagined.

I looked at Emma, my eyes wide with shock. "This changes everything."

"Yeah. What's up with our tutor?"

"I caught him taking the test for someone else today. I almost think he wanted to get caught. When I questioned him, he was ready to confess to the whole scam. Insisted on turning himself in so he could cut a deal."

Now it was her turn to be shocked. "V, we've uncovered something huge. We need to figure out our next move carefully. We're in deep."

A smirk played on my lips. "Careful is my middle name. Let's do some digging. Lucas is a solid lead."

"Or a solid dead end," Emma said. "Do you think he turned himself in yet?"

"Don't know but there's one way to find out," I said. "And I know just who to call."

THE PIECES of the puzzle were almost complete. I had Lucas's confession in my back pocket and Jacob's misdeeds neatly documented. Now for Suzie, the elusive final piece. The road to truth was as intimidating as a tightrope over a canyon. There was just one hitch in my master plan—the road trip to Stanford. Six hours solo? Not exactly a joyride. Plus, there was the minor detail of me, technically, not being legal to chauffeur minors.

Also, let's say I managed to corner Suzie into a confession, what then? March this hot mess to the principal's office, drop it on the College Board's doorstep, or gift-wrap it for the local cops?

Pondering these dilemmas, I called Detective Lomeli, my unofficial mentor in all things legally murky.

"Lomeli," he said, answering his cell.

"Hi Detective, it's V."

"V, what a surprise. To what do I owe the pleasure? Staying out of trouble this year?" Lomeli's voice had that I-know-you're-up-to-something lilt.

"Keeping my nose clean, as always," I replied.

"What's on your mind?"

"I'm in a bit of a bind. Need some legal advice, of sorts."

"Might want to consult a lawyer for that."

"It's not lawyer territory yet. It's more about a certain standardized test and some less-than-standard practices."

"Are we talking cheating on the SATs, here?"

"Yes, sir."

His tone shifted, all business. "That's criminal. You're talking serious fraud and identity theft. The local authorities should definitely be involved. Who are we turning in?"

I hesitated. "No one just yet. I'm still connecting the dots. I have one more lead, and it's a personal one."

There was a beat of silence, and I could practically feel Lomeli's frown. "V, remember what I told you about playing detective?"

"Etched in my memory. But this one is different. One of the suspects is a friend of mine."

He exhaled, a weary sound. "You know the risks, right? You're not a PI, V."

I nodded, even though he couldn't see it. The thought of facing Suzie, not just as a suspect but as a friend, was like staring into a storm. But storms were made to be weathered.

Lomeli's voice anchored me back to reality. "Just be careful, V. Better hand it over to the pros from here."

"Understood," I said, my mind already racing a mile a minute.

When I ended the call, a buzz of anxious energy zapped through me. I quickly filled Emma in and we hatched a plan. She was all in—no hesitation. Best friend? More like partner in crime-solving. Together, we plotted our next move.

Emma speed-packed her duffle, throwing in clothes for both of us. Getting the parents on board for a "chill weekend at Stanford with Suzie" was a breeze. They were cool with it, just said we had to bring someone with more behind-the-wheel experience. Easy. I already had the perfect person in mind. Someone who just hit the big 1-7 and had been legit to drive for over a year. Plus, my parents trusted him. Zack, duh. Who else?

Emma and I showing up to Skaterz on a Saturday afternoon caught Zack totally off guard.

"Yo, Zack," Emma began, her tone persuasive. "We need a favor. It's major."

Laying it all out, Zack's suspicion flipped to excitement. "Wait, so I'm the getaway driver for some undercover SAT heist?" he chuckled, shaking his head. "I'm in. This is gonna be lit."

"Awesome, now he's gonna be annoying," I grumbled, trying not to crack a smile at his reaction.

"But for real, Zack, can you just bail on work like that?" Emma asked.

Zack flashed a sly grin. "Chill, I got this. But, like, maybe don't watch. Catch my drift? Wait in my ride." He flicked his Pathfinder keys at me, that classic Zack smirk playing on his lips.

We watched Zack as he swaggered over to his boss, all confidence. Emma and I shot each other that "can you even believe this?" look, cracking up a bit as the tension of our whole crazy plan seemed to take a backseat to Zack's chill attitude.

Hopping into the Pathfinder, the reality of what we were about to do hit me. *We're actually doing this.* We were on our way to Stanford to confront Suzie, jumping straight into a risky situation.

44
UNMASKING TRUTHS

The drive to Palo Alto was a blur of anticipation and strategy. As Zack's car cruised along the sun-drenched streets, the tall palm trees of Stanford welcomed us, their leaves whispering secrets in the evening breeze. The campus, with its architectural beauty and the scent of eucalyptus in the air, seemed a world away from the turmoil we were about to step into.

We had made the six hour trip with only one brief stop for gas and nature's call. Now it was nearing nightfall, and we were about to confront Suzie Denton on her own turf.

We drove deeper into the campus, the architectural grandeur of Stanford unfolding before us. The red-tiled roofs were dark shapes under the bright moon, and the sandstone buildings with their intricate arches and columns belied their legacy of academic excellence.

"There's the Main Quad," I pointed out, recalling the pictures I'd seen online. The historic buildings, with their ornate façades, surrounded a vast, quiet space.

Zack parked his Pathfinder near the Main Quadrangle, and

we stepped out, stretching our legs. The atmosphere was peaceful at just after seven on a Saturday night. "I'll wait here," he said. "Just in case we need a quick getaway."

"I told you, I booked us a motel room—" I began.

"I know," Zack cut me off. "But we need to be ready for anything. We might have to get back quick."

"Yeah, I guess," I said. "Thanks."

"Don't mention it. Let's just say you owe me one." Zack grinned.

"Right." I smiled back, my palms sweating.

"Can you believe Suzie is part of all this?" Emma asked as we walked away.

I shook my head. "It's hard to imagine her taking such a big risk."

We walked toward the Quad, my eyes taking in the sight of students on the walkways, meandering between the residence halls.

"It's beautiful here," Emma said softly, echoing my thoughts.

"Yeah, it is," I agreed, feeling a pang of sadness for Suzie.

As we approached Suzie's dorm, my heart pounded faster. This was it.

"Ready?" Emma asked, her eyes meeting mine.

I nodded, taking a deep breath. "Let's do this."

I knocked on Suzie's door and braced myself, sucking in a breath of air. "Here we go."

The door opened and a blonde I'd never seen before stared at me expectantly. "Where's my pizza?" She waited, bored.

"Sorry, I think I have the wrong room. I'm looking for Suzie—"

"V? Is that you?" a voice from behind the door called out.

"Yeah, Suzie, it's me," I said. "I brought Emma, too. We wanted to surprise you."

The blonde pushed the door all the way open and motioned us in. "I'm gonna go look for the pizza guy," she said. "I think he's lost again." She left the room.

And then, there we were, Emma and I, in the room with my friend Suzie. The one who had volunteered with pet rescues, helped us get my brother's puppy, Lucky, and had even helped out with Emma's kidnapping case two years ago. The Suzie with mousy, straight brown hair and glasses, who now had honey-blonde highlights and contacts.

She spread her arms out wide. "Come give me a hug," she said, no trace of surprise or warmth in her voice. Holding me close, she whispered, "Here to stab me in the back?"

I pulled away sharply and stared at her, brows furrowed.

"Relax. What's wrong, V? Did you really think I wouldn't know you were coming after me?" She laughed, a bitter sound that echoed in the quiet room. "Give me more credit than that. Do you know how smart I am? I have an IQ of 162. That's above genius level. I'm the best, but they never saw it."

"Why, Suzie? Why throw away your future for this?"

"It's not about the future," Suzie hissed. "It's about the past. About what they did to me."

"What do you mean? Who's 'they'?"

"The system," Suzie spat. "I was the rightful valedictorian. But they cheated me out of it. Gave it to someone else, someone less deserving."

"So, you decided to cheat others?"

"It's not that simple!" Suzie's voice broke, and for a moment, the façade of the untouchable mastermind faltered. "I was perfect. I did everything right. But it wasn't enough. So, I decided to show them their flawed system. To break it."

"By helping others cheat?" I asked softly.

Suzie's eyes flared. "Yes! Let those with less intelligence have their perfect scores. Let the system crumble under the weight of its own hypocrisy."

I sighed. "You could've used your brilliance for so much more."

"I used it for what mattered. For justice. For revenge."

"But at what cost, Suzie? You're caught. It's over."

Suzie's face twisted in a mix of anger and pain. "I know. But I made them listen. I made them see."

"But what did you see, Suzie? In all this, what did you learn about yourself?"

Suzie looked away, her eyes glistening. "That sometimes, the cost of revenge is higher than its satisfaction."

The silence that followed was filled with unspoken words and the weight of imminent consequences. Suzie's confession, raw and unfiltered, was a bitter testimonial to the injustices she faced and the flawed path of vengeance she chose.

The campus police appeared at the open door as my phone chimed.

It was a text from Detective Lomeli.

> Your pal Lucas turned himself in. Sang like a canary. I trust Suzie is in good hands?

> You mean cuffs?

45

REVELATIONS AT REST

A few days later, I chose to accompany Mom to her chemo appointment instead of going to school. It had been too long since we had a proper heart-to-heart, and these sessions often lasted most of the day. I knew she'd be a captive audience, but more than that, I wanted the comfort of her company.

As the nurse finished setting up Mom's IV, I pulled a chair close to her and began unraveling the case I'd been working on all school year.

"So, about the SAT cheating ring I blew wide open . . ." I started, watching her face light up with interest.

Mom adjusted in her chair, a soft smile playing on her lips despite the fatigue in her eyes. "I knew you were onto something big, sweetie. Tell me everything."

I plunged into the story, detailing every twist and turn. "Lucas Bennett, my Prepped tutor, was involved. He got a reduced sentence for turning in evidence against Jacob, Suzie, the other test-takers, and the guys who made the fake school IDs. In total, twenty people were arrested. Can you believe it?"

Her eyes widened. "Twenty? Wow, I had no idea it was so extensive."

"Yeah, and guess what? Suzie Denton was the mastermind. You remember her, right? Top of the class Suzie?"

Mom's expression shifted to one of disbelief. "Suzie? That sweet girl who helped us get Lucky?"

"The very same. She started it as a dare and ended up with a very lucrative scheme, enough to pay her Stanford tuition, and then some. It's crazy."

As I recounted Suzie's fall from grace and the elaborate scheme of scouting clients, Mom's expressions ranged from shock to amusement. When I got to the part about Lucas and the dog treats, she stopped me.

"Wait, slow down. Why was Lucas prowling around our house?"

"Every time a new class of Prepped students started up, he'd scout out where they lived, poking around to see if their parents were rich enough to afford their 'services.' Not wanting to be seen lurking around, or worse yet, get bitten, he lined his pockets with dog treats to bribe a few of the local canine residents. Remember when I told you about the man we saw following us on our walk a while ago? Lucky kept giving him the stink eye and I couldn't figure out why."

"Ah! So that explains Lucky's behavior that day! Who would've thought?" She shook her head, giggling. "It's like something out of a detective novel."

I nodded, grinning. "Exactly! And to think, all this while the clue was right under our noses—well, under Lucky's nose, to be more precise."

"And Jacob?" Mom asked.

"Jacob was tasked with connecting the students willing to pay for guaranteed high test scores with the test-takers, and for getting the fake high school IDs made. Jacob is in deep trouble. I heard something about community service since he's a minor."

Mom reached out, squeezing my hand. "I'm so proud of you, V. Not just for helping to uncover all this, but for how you handled everything. It must have been tough."

I felt a warmth spread through me at her words. "It was, Mom. But I learned a lot. About integrity, and about how far some people will go when they're desperate."

Her grip tightened, her voice soft but firm. "And you've come out stronger for it. Just promise me you'll always use that brilliant mind of yours for good, okay?"

"I promise, Mom." I leaned in, resting my head against her shoulder. In the steady beep of the monitors and the quiet of the room, I felt a sense of calm, not just because I'd solved the case, but something deeper within me. I knew we'd be okay.

AT SCHOOL, the aftermath of the scandal was like being in the eye of a hurricane of emotions and reactions. Some students walked the halls with 'betrayal' etched on their faces, their whispers like gusts of anger and disappointment. Others, recognizing me, offered smiles and nods, their eyes shining with respect and awe.

Principal Fitzgibbon made an announcement over the PA system first thing in the morning, his voice grave but firm. "There will be a full investigation into the SAT cheating scandal," he declared. "Rest assured, there will be consequences for all involved." His words hung heavy in the air, a solemn promise of justice.

As I closed my locker, Emma approached, her steps brisk with purpose. She wrapped an arm around me, her grin wide and proud. "You did it, V. You really did it," she said, her voice vibrant with excitement.

I couldn't help but smile back, feeling a wave of relief wash over me. "We did it," I corrected her gently. "I couldn't have done it without your help, Emma."

"That's what friends are for," she replied, her tone light but sincere.

Curiosity piqued, I nudged the conversation toward a topic we'd been dancing around. "How's your friend Miles Archer taking the news?" I asked.

Emma rolled her eyes but her lips twitched with amusement. "He was shocked, of course. He knew the kids making the fake IDs, but they weren't his friends. He said they got what they deserved." She paused, a hint of red coloring her cheeks. "And he admitted, the only time he even thought about making a fake ID was the one he would've made for me."

I laughed, nudging her playfully. "Wow, he is crushing on you bad. He was willing to commit a crime for you!"

"Gee, thanks," Emma retorted, but she was laughing too.

As we walked through the hall, I could feel the shift in the atmosphere. The secret that had weighed down these halls had been lifted. It was out in the open now, exposed to the light. The cheaters, once hidden in plain sight, were known. It was a victory, yes, but it wasn't without its costs. Friendships had been strained, reputations tarnished, and the illusion of innocence shattered.

But justice had been served, some wrongs had been righted. The truth, harsh and unyielding, had been unveiled, and there was a certain peace in that. As Emma and I reached class, I realized this wasn't just the end of a case, but the beginning of healing and moving forward, for all of us at Sierra High School.

46

UNDER THE STARS

oday was the day. The day I would receive my SAT results. The kitchen was filled with anticipation as I sat at the table, my laptop open before me. Taking a deep breath to steady my nerves, I logged into the SAT portal. Mom, Dad, Grandma, Emma, and even my little brother were gathered around, a circle of support.

Mom's hand rested gently on my shoulder in silent support. Dad and Grandma exchanged anxious glances, while Emma gave me an encouraging thumbs-up. Scotty, not fully grasping the moment's significance, bounced on his toes in excitement.

The screen loaded, and there they were . . . my scores. A 785 on verbal and a 660 on math. A total of 1445. I'd done it. I'd really done it. Better than I hoped. The tension in the room broke like a wave, relief and pride flooding in to take its place.

"Well, I'm no Suzie Denton, but I did all right," I said, unable to keep the grin off my face.

"You did better than 'all right,'" Mom said, her voice thick with emotion. Her eyes were shining, not just with pride, but with something deeper—a recognition of the hurdles I'd overcome. "I knew you would."

"Wow, V. You killed it on verbal!" Emma exclaimed, her smile wide. "Congratulations!"

I turned to her, my heart full. "And I would have bombed math if it hadn't been for you. Thank you so much for all those late-night study sessions."

Grandma, who'd been quietly wiping away a tear, chimed in, "I'm so proud of you, V. You're one smart cookie."

"Thanks, Grandma. Today, I feel pretty smart," I replied, my voice steady despite the emotions swirling inside me.

Then Scotty, in his typical enthusiastic fashion, declared, "Group hug!"

Laughter filled the room as everyone gathered around, with Scotty in the middle. Arms wrapped around each other, the warmth and love of my family enveloped me. It was an incredible feeling. It was the culmination of so much hard work, not just by me but by everyone who had supported me.

At last, my SAT results were in, the case was closed, and I was moving forward, surrounded by the people who mattered most.

"So, what's next for the great detective?" Emma joked, her eyes sparkling with mischief.

I laughed, feeling lighter than I had in months. "A break, for now. But who knows what the future holds? And speaking of future events, want to help me pick out my dress for prom?"

"Of course!" Emma beamed, her enthusiasm infectious. "And I love the theme, don't you?"

"Sure. 'Under the Stars' – Conjures up a colossal celebration of celestial constellations."

"Wow, V," Emma laughed. "You just now think of that off the top of your head?"

"Nah," I admitted. "Saw it on a prom poster."

As our conversation about prom continued, it became clear this moment was more than just closing a chapter. It was a celebration of the journey and an anticipation of the next adventure, wherever it might lead.

THE COUNTDOWN TO prom night at Sierra High was eclipsed by a scandal of academic proportions, with the fallout from the SAT fiasco casting a long shadow over the usual pre-dance excitement. Those who had cheated found themselves facing harsh realities: suspensions, revoked scores, and the mandate to retake the test. Their absence from prom, a direct consequence of their choices, left a bittersweet taste among the student body.

Since I was the one who'd lit the fuse, whispers trailed me like shadows, a not-so-subtle reminder that exposing truths don't always win popularity contests. Naturally, I thought I'd sit this one out. But amid the school's turbulent atmosphere, there was still a haven of joy and acceptance at home.

Mom was somehow the epicenter of festive spirit. Cancer was a relentless thief, but it hadn't managed to steal her zest for life. She wielded her 35 mm camera like a magic wand, capturing fleeting moments and turning them into lasting memories.

She insisted prom was a rite of passage, a chapter in the story you don't skip.

"But I don't have a date," I'd protested, feeling the sting of the school's social dynamics. In the tangled web of Sierra's social ladder, being dateless felt like showing up to a gunfight with a slingshot.

Yet, there was something in her unwavering gaze that said some battles were worth showing up for, date or no date. "Who needs a date these days? Go with Emma!" she'd declared, accepting no argument.

So Emma and I dressed up, reveling in the ritual of preparing for a milestone event. Dad drove us to a picturesque park, where a quaint bridge arched gracefully over a serene creek. There, among the lush greenery and the gentle murmur of the water, we transformed into models at a photo shoot, laughing and posing as Mom directed us with a photographer's eye and a mother's heart.

"That's it. Work it, baby. Own it. You go, girls. Ah, that's it. Big smiles. Gorgeous!" she encouraged, her enthusiasm undimmed by fatigue.

In those moments, with Mom clicking away, her joy infectious, the weight of her illness seemed to lift, if only temporarily. Her laughter, mingling with ours, created a symphony of happiness I wished could last forever.

Capturing these snapshots of memories was more than just collecting a few keepsakes of prom; they were tokens of love, resilience, and the beauty of the present moment. They were reminders that even amid life's most challenging trials, there were interludes of pure joy.

Mom was fully in her element, her love and vitality imprinting themselves on every photo. And as we headed to prom, with her blessings and laughter echoing in our ears, I knew these memories would be a beacon of light in the days to come.

THE ROYAL PALMS COUNTRY CLUB was transformed into a celestial wonderland, its grounds lit by twinkling lights that mimicked the night sky. As Emma and I approached the entrance, I felt a flutter of nerves. This was my first public appearance since the SAT scandal, and I knew all eyes would be on me.

Emma, ever the rock in my turbulent sea, sensed my apprehension. "You look stunning, V. Don't let anyone's nonsense ruin our night," she said, her voice firm yet reassuring.

She was right. Tonight was about us, not them. I drew a deep breath, feeling the silk of my deep purple dress brush against my skin. It was a bold choice, the color rich and royal, contrasting beautifully with my long, curly auburn hair cascading over my shoulders in loose waves. The dress hugged my figure before flaring out at the waist, its skirt billowing gently in the evening breeze.

Emma, in her periwinkle blue dress, was a vision. The color complemented her luxurious black hair and warm brown complexion perfectly. Her dress, with its elegantly fitted bodice and flowing skirt, sparkled under the starlit projections, making her look like she'd stepped out of a dream.

As we entered the prom, the murmurs and music blended into a low hum. I could feel the weight of stares, some curious, some hostile. Whispers filled the air, their words indistinct but their intention clear. I braced myself, lifting my chin high. I wasn't going to let their judgment define me.

The entire venue was breathtaking. Starlit projections danced across the ceiling, crafting an ethereal canopy that mimicked the night sky. The celestial decor, coupled with the gentle strains of music, created a dreamlike, romantic ambiance.

"Wow, they went all out," Emma murmured beside me, her voice hushed in reverence. Her eyes, wide with wonder, mirrored the twinkling lights above.

"Yeah, it's beautiful," I agreed, my anxiety ebbing away as I took in the enchanting scenery.

We made our way through the crowd, some of our classmates offering small nods or tight smiles. Others turned away, their disdain unhidden. But among the cold shoulders, a few genuine smiles reached us, reminding me not everyone saw me as the villain in their high school drama.

"Let's get some photos," Emma suggested, pulling me toward the beautifully lit photo area, where a backdrop of a star-filled cosmos awaited.

As we struck poses, Emma laughed, pure and uninhibited. It was infectious; soon, I found myself laughing along, the sound mingling with the music and lights around us. My dress seemed to transform, becoming a shield against the whispers and stares. For those moments, in the flash of the camera, I felt liberated.

Eventually, we drifted toward the dance floor after pictures, the music's rhythm embracing us, inviting us to forget the world. For a fleeting moment, it was just us, the music, and the illusion of being lost in a galaxy far away.

Then, a familiar voice in my ear, "May I cut in?" Zack asked.

My heart skipped, then steadied.

"Hi Zack, where's Malia?" I asked, struggling to keep my voice even.

"She's around," he replied with casual indifference. "Don't worry, I told her I wanted to dance with you. She's cool with it."

"Really?" My eyebrow arched in suspicion.

"V, she's not the villain here. Things just happened between us. And there's more you should know."

I waited, a sense of foreboding settling in. "What would that be?"

"As soon as school ends, Malia's moving to San Francisco."

"So? I already knew that."

"Yeah, but . . . her dad got my mom a job there, so we're moving, too."

The news hit me like a quiet storm. "Oh," was all I managed, feeling the room spin slightly.

"Yeah." Zack's voice carried a mix of apology and inevitability. "Mom wanted a fresh start, you know, after Amanda."

"What about Amanda's daughters, the twins?" The question slipped out before I could stop it, and I chastised myself for still caring but I had to know.

He brightened at this. "Actually, funny thing. David was really struggling with the whole 'single dad' thing, and it was too much for his parents to take care of the girls, so Malia's dad got David a job, too. He'll live nearby and now Mom gets to help raise her grandkids."

"That's good. I bet she's excited," I said, my voice barely above a whisper.

He smiled, a touch of old warmth in his eyes. "Mom's ecstatic. She says she's 'over the moon.'"

I pulled away, a laugh that felt more like a shard of glass escaping my lips. "Everything's falling into place for you, isn't it? How convenient." My words were bitter. "Now you won't have to dump her when she leaves."

"Look, V, I'm sorry. I just thought you deserved to hear it from me."

"Thanks, Zee. Really. Enjoy your life up there." My voice was steady, but inside, a storm was brewing. I slipped away from his grasp, escaping to the sanctuary of the ladies' room as fast as I could. I leaned against the sink, allowing a few tears to break free, their trails feeling like the release of a pent-up storm. I couldn't let Zack, or anyone else, see me cry.

It wasn't long before Emma found me. Her presence was a steadfast anchor. "You okay?" she asked, her voice soft in the echoing space.

I nodded, wiping away a few errant tears. "Yeah. Let's go back out there."

We re-entered the prom, and the music and lights enveloped me once more. I felt a newfound resolve stirring within. I wasn't just V—the snitch, the outcast, the girl who'd been dumped. Nor was I just the daughter of a mother fighting cancer. Tonight, I was a girl at her prom, dancing the night away.

The whispers and stares hadn't vanished, but they seemed distant now, muffled under the celestial theme and the rhythm of the music. In that space, under the starlit illusions, I found a sliver of peace. Amid the dancing figures, I let myself get lost in the moment, each step a dance away from the shadows of the past.

I was V, at my prom. And for now, that was enough.

About two weeks later, I did something I hadn't done since I was eleven when Mom used to make me write thank you cards to my relatives for birthday and Christmas presents. . . . I got out a few sheets of my mom's floral stationery and I sat down to write a letter. I didn't edit my thoughts, just poured out my heart, unfiltered and raw.

Dear Brylee,

Hey, how's life in Argentina? I hope this letter finds you well at the University of Buenos Aires, and that you're finally getting the happiness you deserve. I must admit, I've been pretty lousy at keeping in touch. Emma fills me in now and then, and from what I gather, your adventures sound like a dream come true.

You might be wondering why I'm reaching out to you, especially in such an old-fashioned way via snail mail—and a handwritten letter at that. The truth is, you've always had a knack for listening, for understand-

ing, without judgment. Right now, I could really use someone like that. Emma's swamped with her soccer commitments—she's headed to UNC on a full-ride, can you believe it? And as for Zack . . . well, we're no longer together. So here I am, penning my thoughts to someone who once called me a friend.

Miss Torres, my English teacher from last year, has been a guiding light through some recent tough times. She suggested I start a journal, to navigate through the maze of my emotions. It's been a surprisingly therapeutic journey, but a journal can only do so much. It's a solitary act, and right now, I'm craving connection, a need to share with someone who's a bit removed from the chaos of my life.

So, here I am, turning to you. Please don't feel any pressure to respond. Just knowing that these words have reached you, that they've been heard in some way, brings me comfort. I'm about to share something heavy, something that's been weighing on my heart. I guess it's my way of trying not to drown in this sea of grief that's been threatening to engulf me.

Okay here it goes . . .

I never imagined I'd be writing something like this. Each word feels heavier than the last, each sentence a struggle to put together. I guess you've probably heard by now, but the news about my mom . . . it's the worst we could have gotten.

Last Tuesday, we found out the cancer has spread to her brain. She had an MRI of her brain in the morning and then more scans in the afternoon. I wasn't there with her, but Dad was. Dr. Khatri, her oncologist, came by while Mom was still in the scans. Dad had to hear the news alone. When Mom was wheeled out, he couldn't hide the devastation on his face. She told me his first words were, "It wasn't good." Mom asked him, "How long?"

They got in the car, drove to a quiet place, and that's where Dad shared what Dr. Khatri had said. The longest Mom might have is until around Labor Day —maybe four months. Just writing this feels surreal, like it's happening to someone else, not us.

When my parents got home that day, we had the hardest family talk ever. Mom and Dad were honest with Scotty and me. We all cried, held each other, and felt like our world was collapsing. Mom talked about how losing a parent shapes you, changes who you become. She reminded us that she will always be a part of us, that her love doesn't die with her.

The way Mom and Dad have been with each other these past few months . . . it's been heartbreaking but also kind of beautiful. Their love is so deep, so real. I see it in the way Dad lines up her meds, the way they look at each other. Mom says she falls in love with him a thousand times a day. Dad jokes it's because of the meds, but I know it's more than that.

Despite the sadness, she says she still finds joy in the little things. She took a bazillion pictures of Emma and me for prom. I've enclosed one here just for fun.

That was a good day. At the time, she said, "I want to be here for all of your milestones. . . . Another reason to fight and hang onto this beautiful life."

Brylee, I believed her! I thought we had more time. She says she wants to make more fun memories, so she can leave us with smiles as well as tears.

The pain she's going through is hard to see. She's fighting it, trying to stay strong. And in those moments, she talks about wanting to prove science wrong. She wants to fight and live and hold onto every-thing. Sometimes, she even has me believing that, against all odds, she's going to somehow beat it. Wouldn't that be something if she did?

Thanks for listening, Brylee.

I miss you.

Your friend,
Violet

FOREVER STARS

Book Four in the
CHRONICLES *of V series*
coming soon!

As the dawn of her senior year at Sierra High School breaks, V confronts challenges far beyond the usual stress of college admissions and essays. With the winds of change stirring, she finds herself at a crossroads, shadowed by the weight of heartache and emptiness. Within this emotional turmoil, a startling revelation surfaces—a secret so profound it threatens to unravel everything she knows.

Faced with what could be her most critical and defining case, V must navigate a path where every decision holds the power to change destinies. *Forever Stars* transcends the realm of mystery, testing the limits of trust, friendship, and the strength of a young detective on the brink of her greatest challenge.

The stakes have soared to new heights, emotions run raw, and the quest for bravery is paramount. Join V as she navigates the intricate web of secrets and lies, where the light of truth battles the shadows of doubt, promising an adventure that will leave readers breathless.

THANK YOU

Your journey through **Broken Stars** means the world to me. If V's story has touched you, consider staying connected through our monthly newsletter. Not only will you receive book updates and promos, you'll also get two exclusive short stories that expand V's world, prequels to book 1, **Glass Stars**. Discover more at **taschelaine.com**.

Your words matter! A review from you is like a star guiding other readers to V's world. If you could take a moment to share your thoughts on Goodreads or your favorite review site, it would be immensely appreciated. Just a few heartfelt words are more than enough.

Want a signed copy of *Broken Stars* or any of my other books? Visit our Lil Book Shop for your own personalized edition.

V, her friends (the stars of the story!), and I thank you from the bottom of our hearts!

Want to stay connected? Follow me on Instagram (@Tasches) or TikTok (@TascheLaine) for daily updates, insights, and a peek into my writing world!

Acknowledgments

From the depths of my heart, I extend my profound appreciation to Kim Wilch, my Alpha reader, whose spot-on insights and eagle-eyed scrutiny have been indispensable. Kim, your keen observations and unwavering dedication have left an indelible mark on this work.

A heartfelt salute to the artistic maestros at 100 Covers (100covers.com). Your talent and vision have clothed my words in a cover that speaks volumes, capturing the essence of V's journey beautifully.

To Tiana, my youth expert! Thank you for guiding me through the intricacies of "teen-speak," ensuring V's story resonates with authenticity and relevance. Your ability to keep my references sharp has been the backbone of this project's success.

My ARC team deserves a universe of thanks for their early reviews and relentless efforts to propel this book into the hearts and hands of readers. Your enthusiasm and support for this series are the winds beneath V's wings—I truly would be adrift without you.

To my #1 fan and the best Beta reader a writer could ever wish for, Kim Damato—Mom. Your belief in my dreams has been my guiding light. Thank you for reading every word I've written—all the way from my earliest scribbles about whimsical cats. My love for you knows no bounds; to the stars and infinity—forever.

And to you, dear reader, my final words of gratitude. Your journey with V, your eagerness to turn each page, and your companionship through every twist and turn have been the greatest gifts of all. I hope you've found joy and adventure in these pages and that you'll stay by our side as we conclude this series. Your presence makes every word worthwhile.

ALSO BY TASCHE LAINE

CLOSURE: Based On A True Story

CHAMELEON: A Domestic Thriller

SHORT STORY COLLECTIONS

WINDS of WINTER

WINGS of PROPHECY

CHRONICLES OF V

GLASS STARS

BRIGHT STARS

BROKEN STARS

FOREVER STARS

CHILDREN'S SERIES

Get Up, Lil Peter. Get Up!

You Can't Quit, Lil Peter, You Just Can't

Teamwork, Lil Peter, It Works

Pick Me, Lil Peter, Pick Me

Small Things, Lil Peter, Make A Big Difference

Smile Lil Peter, It's A Gift

Your Word, Lil Peter, Is Your Word

Be True, Lil Peter, Be You

ABOUT THE AUTHOR

Tasche Laine is a versatile author with a rich background in journalism, teaching, and book editing. Her award-winning works include *Closure* and *Chameleon*, showcasing her talent in crafting compelling narratives. She also delves into the young adult genre with her engaging series, *Chronicles of V*, and reaches younger audiences through the children's series, *Lil Peter*, co-written with her husband, Peter Valdez.

Now residing in the serene landscapes of the Pacific Northwest, Tasche finds joy and inspiration in her life with her husband and their adorable pups, Story and Page. Her connections to southern California remain strong, serving as a haven for hugs and sunshine. Tasche's writing journey, fueled by diverse experiences and a passion for storytelling, reflects in her dynamic range of work.

For a deeper dive into Tasche Laine's world, visit her website at taschelaine.com.

instagram.com/tasches

tiktok.com/@taschelaine

facebook.com/TascheLaine

goodreads.com/tasche_laine

amazon.com/author/taschelaine

bookbub.com/authors/tasche-laine